SWEET SATURDAYS

PAMELA M. KELLEY

PIPING PLOVER PRESS

INTRODUCTION

Quinn Jacobs hasn't had a serious relationship in a long time. He's too busy running the family business, Bakey's--a nationwide bakery chain. He's only in town to get the newest store up and running. But he has noticed the woman in the cottage next to his

And Paula O'Neill has noticed him too. It's hard not to. Like her, he leaves for work early, and comes home late. Paula has a busy job at a local marketing agency but her favorite day of the week is Saturday when she works at her aunt's bakery, decorating cakes. When her aunt announces that she is retiring and wants Paula to take over the business, she is thrilled. Everything in her life is going so well. She's even started spending time with her new neighbor Quinn, who is funny and sweet and says that the area is growing on him.

But there's one big problem, Quinn hasn't exactly

shared what his family's business is with Paula, and Bakey's is going to be opening right across the street from her aunt's bakery. When they've opened in other locations, competing businesses haven't always survived. Will this kill their chance at romance too?

INDIGO BAY SWEET ROMANCE SERIES

A multi author sweet romance series

Sweet Saturdays, Pamela M. Kelley
Sweet Beginnings, Melissa McClone
Sweet Starlight, Kay Correll
Sweet Forgiveness, Jean Oram
Sweet Reunion, Stacy Claflin
Sweet Entanglement, Jean Gordon

Earlier books in the series

Sweet Dreams, Stacy Claflin
Sweet Matchmaker, Jean Oram
Sweet Sunrise, Kay Correll
Sweet Illusions, Jeanette Lewis
Sweet Regrets, Jennifer Peel
Sweet Rendezvous, Jennifer Stewart

Holiday books

Sweet Holiday Surprise, Jean Oram
Sweet Holiday Memories, Kay Correll
Sweet Holiday Wishes, Melissa McClone
Sweet Holiday Traditions, Danielle Stewart

CHAPTER 1

Paula O'Neill dipped a bare toe in the sand and wondered if she had time for a walk along the beach before Aunt Tessa arrived. She'd called earlier and wanted to stop by for a chat. Her aunt had sounded excited, but was also somewhat evasive and said that it was too important to discuss over the phone.

She decided to wait until later, in case Aunt Tessa showed up early, which she sometimes did. It was a beautiful evening, not quite six thirty, and the air was still warm. She went inside and poured a glass of sweet tea before coming back out to the porch. She sat in her favorite spot, the corner of a comfy padded love seat that that was also a rocker.

She never tired of the view. She'd bought this beachfront cottage three years ago and loved it at first sight. It was a small house, just two bedrooms, but it had all the space she needed, including a small balcony off her bedroom and the farmer's porch. She took her coffee on the porch most mornings if she wasn't running late for work. And she sometimes enjoyed a glass of wine there, too, at the end of a long day.

She sipped her iced tea as she watched the waves crash on the beach, boats far out on the water and people strolling by. A cool breeze ruffled her hair, and she caught a whiff of the ocean's salty scent. Indigo Bay was her happy place, where she relaxed and re-energized. She'd been thrilled when one of the cottages became available and she was able to buy. It was a great neighborhood, a mixture of year-round residents and rental cottages.

Paula's neighbor on her right, Hope, had become one of her best friends. She was an artist, and they'd clicked instantly. The cottage on the other side was a rental and there was a steady stream of new people coming and going. Paula hadn't met the newest tenant yet, but she'd seen him drive in a few days ago as she was heading off to work. She was mildly curious about him as it was unusual to have a single younger man staying there. Usually it was families or groups of friends.

She turned at the sound of a car door closing and saw her aunt coming her way.

"That sweet tea looks good." Aunt Tessa wiped her brow as she stepped onto the porch. Paula jumped up and gave her a hug.

"Have a seat. I'll pour you a glass."

She returned a moment later carrying a tall glass of iced tea with a slice of lemon and set it on the matching white wicker coffee table.

"Thanks, honey. I do love it here, but it sure does get hot." It was a typical low country evening. The air was still thick and warm, the humidity high. Aunt Tessa looked elegant as usual, though, in her pale yellow linen top and matching pants. A triple string of pearls pulled the look together. Her hair fell just below her chin in a perfectly shaped lemony bob, reminding Paula that she was overdue for a trim.

Her aunt's blue-gray eyes found Paula's.

"I've made a decision. It involves you, which is why I dragged myself out here."

Paula nodded and waited.

"I know you've always loved helping in the shop," Aunt Tessa began.

Paula smiled. Saturdays were her favorite day of the week. Even after graduating from college and business school and joining an up-and-coming advertising agency, she still spent most Saturdays working at The Sweet Shop, her aunt's bakery. They made all kinds of baked goods and were known for their wedding cakes.

"And I know you've mentioned wanting to run your own business some day. You never did say what kind of business that might be. Have you decided?"

Paula shook her head. "No. I've been so busy at the agency, and I enjoy it. I've learned a lot there." She helped local businesses with their advertising and social media marketing strategy. The work was usually interesting and varied.

Aunt Tessa smiled, put her hand over Paula's and gave it a squeeze. "Well, my dear. The perfect solution has come to me. I'd like to have you take over The Sweet Shop if you're interested. You can pay me a small percentage of the profits, if that works for you."

Paula's jaw dropped. This was the last thing she would have expected. She'd always assumed that her aunt would run The Sweet Shop until she dropped.

"I'm honored that you'd think of me for it. But, is everything okay? You're not sick or anything?" Aunt Tessa looked as healthy as could be, but it just didn't make sense otherwise. She was barely seventy and one of the most active people she knew.

Her aunt laughed. "No, honey, I'm not sick. I'm just tired of working. I'm done. I'm ready to move on to the next chapter and I know if you take over, it will be in good hands. And you know how I sometimes just know things?"

Paula nodded. Aunt Tessa had a bit of a reputation in the family for being eerily intuitive.

"Well, I know you can do this," she said with absolute certainty.

A feeling of excitement swept through Paula. She'd mentioned different marketing ideas to her aunt over the years, but Aunt Tessa had never wanted to try them. Paula's mind raced with all the various things she could do. She spent most of her time on Saturdays working with special order cakes. Now she could do that all the time and wouldn't have to go into an office every day. The thought was very appealing.

"When are you thinking of making the change?"

Her aunt's eyes lit up and held a hint of mischief. "A month from now, ideally. That's when your mother and I are leaving for our cruise."

"What cruise?" This was the first Paula was hearing about it.

"Oh, didn't I mention it? We're going around the British Isles and it's a theater cruise. There will be lectures on the ship and we'll be attending all kinds of shows in London. It's going to be marvelous."

"What about Dad?" Paula wondered aloud.

"Oh, he doesn't mind at all. He's going to hold down the fort. Someone has to run the store, after all." Paula's father had a thriving business at the local marina. His general store was always busy, and it was right around the corner from Sweet Caroline's Cafe, where he had his breakfast almost every day before making his way to the store around ten. His manager, Stacy, opened bright and early most mornings for him.

"Are you sure about this? I could probably just take some time off and cover the shop for you while you're away?" As tempted as Paula was, she wanted to make sure her aunt had really thought this through. She did have a tendency to be impulsive at times.

"Oh, I'm as sure as I could ever be. I've been thinking about this for a long time." She bit her lip and looked worried for a moment. "I'll be honest with you, honey. I just don't think I have it in me to go up against Bakey's. They sent me another letter, with a better offer, or so they said."

"Bakey's made you an offer? Are you sure you don't want to take it?" Paula knew her aunt had been upset when she'd learned the nationwide bakery was planning to open a huge new store right across the street from The Sweet Shop. They both knew that in other parts of the country, other smaller bakeries hadn't survived when Bakey's came to town. They priced lower than the competition, and Paula had to admit their products were good. She'd had Bakey's donuts and pastries when she'd gone to Savannah where they were headquartered.

"I'd rather not! Unless you really don't like the idea of taking over the shop? It would kill me to sell to them. But I just don't have the energy to fight them. I'd love to see you do it."

Paula smiled. "If you're sure, then I'd love to do it, too. I have lots of ideas for how we can market to win new business. We already have a better product and loyal customers."

"That we do. So, it's settled then? You'll give your notice and start in a month." Her aunt glanced at her watch and stood. "I have to be off. I'm meeting the girls for supper." The 'girls' were four of her aunt's closest friends. They got together often for dinner.

Her aunt left and Paula decided to go for a run. She needed to burn off some energy and her mind whirled with the all the possibilities for taking over the store.

"How's the cottage? Is it as pretty as I remember?"

Quinn Jacobs smiled at his grandmother's question. She was only a few hours away, in Savannah, most likely calling from her corner office at Bakey's corporate headquarters, where she'd been in charge for over thirty years. He leaned against the porch railing and glanced back at the pale green cottage with its snow white shutters and trim and the welcoming window boxes overflowing with pink flowers.

"It's perfect, Gram. Thank you for insisting I come a few weeks early and take some vacation time." He could almost imagine his grandmother's satisfied smile.

"You haven't taken any real time off in over a year. You'll be busy soon enough with the store opening, so you might as well enjoy all that Indigo Bay has to offer until then. Didn't you once tell me that you wanted to learn how to surf?"

Quinn laughed. "I did. I'm not sure if this area is known for it's surfing, though."

"Well, go kayaking then or that new thing, what is it? Paddle boarding! That's it. Looks like a surfboard. That looks fun."

"Actually, that's not a bad idea." Quinn had noticed a surf shop further up the beach. He could probably rent a board for an afternoon.

"Now, I don't want to hear that you're working for the next two weeks. I'm getting daily reports from Marshall, and everything is on schedule. We'll need you there when it gets closer to opening day. We sent a new offer off to that Tessa woman and I'm confident that she'll accept."

"The little bakery across the street? You think that's all set?" Quinn hoped so. It was always easier if they were able to buy out nearby competitors instead of taking them on directly. He knew it was just business, but it was one aspect that he'd never felt good about. He much preferred when they were able to come to an agreement that both sides felt was a win.

His grandmother was quiet for a moment and Quinn sensed that it wasn't fully settled. "Well, not yet. But it's a very good offer. She should take it!"

Quinn sighed. "I'll stop in there and check the place out this week."

"Well, if you do, just go in as a customer. We still haven't heard back yet, so I don't want you to say anything too soon. Besides, you're on vacation. No working!" She sounded so fierce that he laughed again.

"Okay, no working," he agreed and promised to check in toward the end of the week. He hung up and decided to take a walk down the beach and see if the surf shop was still open. Maybe he'd line up a board for the next day. He had no plans for the rest of the week besides relaxing on the beach, firing up the grill occasionally and heading into town to do some exploring.

As he stepped off his porch onto the sandy pathway to the beach, he noticed his neighbor jogging toward him. She slowed to a walk as she got closer and he couldn't help admiring her long, lean muscles, which her baby blue tank top and shorts showed off. Her hair was in a long ponytail, the color so dark it was almost black. Yet her skin was fair and there was a smattering of freckles across her cute nose. Her eyes were a pretty shade of blue—or was it gray? She smiled when she reached him and held out her hand.

"Hi. I'm your next door neighbor, Paula O'Neill. I noticed you drive in the other day as I was heading off to work." He shook her hand and liked the feel of her smooth, soft skin against his.

"Nice to meet you, Paula. I'm Quinn. I'll be around for the next few weeks."

"Oh, are you taking a vacation?"

He laughed. "Yes. My grandmother insisted that I take the next two weeks off. I suppose I don't do that often enough."

Paula smiled. "You must like your job."

"I do, actually. It's a family business and I work for my grandmother."

"That's nice!" She seemed to hesitate for a moment before saying, "I work in marketing at a local ad agency. So, what do you have planned for your vacation? I can suggest some local restaurants."

"No plans other than relaxing. I'd love some suggestions."

"Well, for breakfast, you have to go to Sweet Caroline's. It's the local hangout. My father is there every morning with his cronies, solving all the world's problems over coffee." She smiled when she mentioned her father.

"I'll be sure to check that out, thanks." He'd probably head there in the morning as he hadn't stocked up on groceries yet.

"There's a general store right around the corner from there, too, at the marina. It's actually my dad's shop." Quinn figured he might as well stop in there, too, after breakfast and pick up a few things.

"Where's your favorite place to go for dinner?" He wondered if she was single. He'd recently turned thirty-four and guessed her age to be close to his, maybe a few years younger.

"For dinner? Well, there's a great place just a short walk from here. The Surf Shack. It's casual and beachy. Fried seafood, fresh fish. Burgers."

He smiled. "I'll have to check that out soon. Maybe you'll come along sometime? I don't know a soul here," he admitted. He found her attractive, but if she wasn't interested, he'd still welcome her company.

"Oh, sure," she said, and then added, "I could see

if Hope and her brother, Von, want to join us, too. She lives on the other side of me."

"Sure. The more the merrier." He'd prefer to just go with Paula and get to know her better, but if she wanted to bring her neighbor, that was fine by him, too.

"Okay. Well, it was nice to meet you. I should probably head in."

"Have a good night. And stop by anytime if you feel like company. If I'm not home, I'll probably be at the beach. Or paddle-boarding."

"I keep meaning to try that. It looks like so much fun."

"I haven't tried it yet, either, but it's on my agenda for tomorrow."

Paula laughed. "Have fun."

CHAPTER 2

Quinn slept until almost nine the next morning, and his stomach was grumbling as he eased out of bed and made his way into the bathroom for a quick shower. By the time he dressed and towel-dried his hair, the grumbling had turned into a roar. He drove the short distance to Sweet Caroline's Cafe and slid into one of the few empty seats along the busy counter.

An older but still very pretty woman, with stylish brown hair walked over to him holding a menu and a full pot of coffee. Quinn quickly turned over the empty cup that marked his spot and nodded. The woman smiled and handed him a menu as she poured.

"Welcome to Sweet Caroline's. I'm Caroline. Specials are up on the board. If you're hungry, you can't go wrong with the kitchen sink omelet. Do you need a few minutes to look over the menu?" He looked at the omelet description, written in blue chalk. It contained chopped ham, bacon, mushrooms, onions, peppers, cheddar cheese and potatoes.

"No. I'll have the omelet, with white toast and a large orange juice."

"I'll put it right in." Caroline whisked his menu away and returned a moment later with his juice. He took a sip and glanced around the busy restaurant. It was a mix of families and what looked like regulars. He noticed a small group of older men at the opposite end of the counter and wondered if one of them was Paula's father. Their plates were mostly empty, but they were still sipping coffee and engaged in a lively discussion.

Just as Caroline set his breakfast down, someone sat on the stool beside him.

"Looks like my mom is treating you well."

Quinn turned and saw that it was Dallas. He was about his age and owned the cottage he was renting, along with a bunch of others.

"I didn't realize that was your mom. This place is great." Quinn reached for the ketchup as he cut into the omelet and took his first bite.

"Do you want your usual, honey?" Caroline asked her son.

Dallas yawned. "Yes, thanks. I'll have a side of bacon, too."

Caroline raised one eyebrow. "Late night?"

He grinned. "A few of us were at the Surf Shack until closing. It was a good time."

Caroline shook her head as she walked off to put her son's order in.

"Is that the place right up the road from the cottages? Walking distance?" Quinn asked.

"That's it. You should come with us one of these nights while you're in town. It's a fun place, and the food is pretty good, too."

"Thanks. I might take you up on that. I don't have any plans for the next few weeks other than relaxing."

Dallas yawned again and reached for his coffee. "Well, you're in the right place then."

"I met one of my neighbors last night. Paula. Do you know her?"

"Sure, I know Paula. She bought her place a few years ago. I don't know her well, though. She works a lot. I've seen her and Hope, who lives next to her, at the Surf Shack occasionally. They're both really nice girls. You interested?"

Was he? "Just curious. I'm only here for a few weeks."

"You live in Savannah, though, right? That's not too far." Depending on traffic, it was less than two hours away.

"Technically, that's where I live. But I haven't spent much time there in the past few years. I'm usually on the road, all over the country, wherever we're opening a new location."

"Do you like traveling that much? I hate leaving

the beach. I'm always eager to get home the few times a year I go away."

"I don't mind it. I'm used to it by now. You ever see that movie with George Clooney, Up in the Air? That's me."

Dallas frowned as his mother set down an overflowing plate of French toast. He spread whipped butter across the top and then drowned it in maple syrup. "Isn't that the movie where he flies around firing people?" he asked as he cut a big bite of French toast.

"Yeah, that's the one. Of course, I'm not firing anyone." Caroline topped off his coffee after she cleared away his empty plate.

"Good. I thought that was a depressing movie. The guy's apartment looked like a hotel room. There was nothing in it."

Quinn pictured his home in Savannah. His grandmother had once said that it looked like no one lived there. He'd taken it as a compliment at the time. He liked things kept tidy and since he traveled so much, he'd never taken the time to fill it with a lot of stuff. He hated clutter, and had always liked the spare, minimal look. But he had to admit, it had a cold feeling, not unlike a hotel room.

"I like the way you've decorated the cottage. Are the water colors on the wall from a local artist?" The cottage was anything but cold. He'd been struck by the calm, welcoming and colorful decor.

"Yes. It's someone Hope knows. She's an

artist, too."

"No kidding. Maybe I'll have to see about buying one of those paintings before I leave. My apartment could use a little more color."

"I'll see about organizing a group night out—you, me, Paula, Hope, and a few other locals. You can ask Hope about her friend's paintings then. She may know other people to refer you to as well."

"That would be great." He'd also get to spend more time with Paula, too.

"She's single, by the way," Dallas added.

"Who is?"

"Paula. I'm not sure about Hope. She may be, too."

Caroline came by and set Quinn's bill down. "No rush on this." She glanced at Dallas. "You look like you're up to no good. What are you planning?"

Dallas laughed. "Just trying to make sure everyone gets introduced and has a good time."

Caroline smiled. "Sometimes I think my son is the mayor of Indigo Bay—he seems to know what everyone is up to."

"Just taking after you. Everyone tells you their secrets."

Caroline laughed. "They really do."

Quinn paid his tab and left a generous tip. He thanked Caroline and said goodbye to Dallas. As he walked out, he noticed that the group of older men were gone. He decided to head over to the marina's general store and pick up a few things.

Paula breathed in the satisfying smell of melting chocolate. She never tired of it. As soon as it was ready, she dipped a spoon into the chocolate and then drizzled a thin stream of it across the top of the cake she was working on, making zig zag ribbons over mounds of whipped cream. The cake was vanilla, filled with raspberry cream. It was for a surprise fiftieth birthday party being thrown by one of their best clients.

A few minutes later, the scent of sweet vanilla filled the room as Barbara, her aunt's right hand assistant, took a large sheet cake out of the oven. She was a tiny woman, in her mid-fifties, with short blonde hair and tons of energy. Barbara had worked at the shop for over ten years. She was the first one in every morning, arriving by five to start making the day's bread, muffins, and pastries before the shop opened at seven.

"Is Tessa stopping in today?" Barbara asked. Saturdays were Aunt Tessa's one day off, but she often popped in if she was out and about.

"She said she might try to come by after lunch."

Barbara glanced out the window at the store across the street, the site of the new Bakey's. Paula followed her gaze and saw a stream of construction workers heading back inside after their mid-morning coffee break.

"It looks like they're moving along fast over there."

Barbara shook her head. "I don't know why they had to open up so close to us. Doesn't seem right."

"The space came available and we've already proven that it's a good spot for a bakery," Paula said. She didn't like it either, but she understood it was a good business decision.

Barbara frowned. "Good for one. For two? I don't know."

Paula had the same concern but didn't want to worry Barbara.

"We'll be fine. We have a good client base and people love our products. We may need to do some more marketing, though."

"Your aunt has never been keen on spending money on advertising," Barbara said.

Paula knew that her aunt wanted to tell Barbara herself about Paula taking over the shop, so she just said, "I think she might be coming around on that."

When a rush of customers came in at once, Paula went to the front of the store to help Julia at the counter. Julia was a high school student and worked part-time on the weekends. She waited on customers and ran the register.

There was a lull around eleven thirty and Paula was about to go back into the kitchen to work on another custom order when the front door chimed and a familiar face walked in. Her new neighbor, Quinn. He looked surprised to see her.

"I didn't know you worked here, too."

"My aunt owns the shop. I help her out on Saturdays so she gets a day off," Paula explained.

"That's nice of you."

Paula smiled. "I've been doing it for years. I always look forward to Saturdays."

Quinn glanced around the store. "It smells pretty good in here."

"What are you in the mood for? The breads are great. If you want something sweet, you can't go wrong with the cannoli."

"Oh? She makes a good cannoli? I haven't had one of those in ages."

"Hers will make you think you're in Italy. It's that good. Do you want it plain or dipped in chocolate chips?"

"Chocolate, of course. I'll take a half-dozen. One for now and the rest for later."

Paula noticed Quinn roaming around the shop while she got his cannoli shells. He seemed impressed as he glanced at the display cases full of pastries and fresh-baked bread. She filled a pastry bag with the sweet ricotta cream filling, piped it into the cannoli cookie shells, then dipped the ends into a dish of mini chocolate chips. She packed five of them into a thin cardboard box and handed the sixth to him in a little paper bag.

"Would you like anything else?" she asked.

"Sure. I'll have a loaf of white bread, too." He took a bite of the cannoli as she rang him up.

"This is excellent." He handed her his credit card and took another big bite.

Paula was pleased by his expression. She'd mixed the cannoli filling earlier that morning. It was one of her favorite desserts, too.

"I had breakfast at Sweet Caroline's this morning and stopped by your father's shop after. We chatted for a bit. He said the surfing is good about a mile down the beach."

"He did? I didn't know my father paid attention to that." He'd never mentioned surfing before.

Quinn laughed. "He said he tried it years ago. It wasn't for him, but he said he knew the best spot. I'm going to give it a shot this afternoon. Wish me luck!"

"I'm sure you'll do great. That sounds like fun."

"Well, if I figure it out, I'll teach you, if you're interested."

She laughed, trying to picture it. "We'll see about that."

"What time do you have to work until?" Quinn asked.

"We close at three so not too long after that."

"You probably have plans already, but if not, I was thinking of walking over to the Surf Shack for dinner. I ran into Dallas at breakfast and he said we should all go sometime."

Paula had plans to see a friend later, but received a message from her a few hours ago cancelling. So, she was tempted to join Quinn.

"That sounds like fun. I'd love to."

He looked pleasantly surprised. "Great, I'll knock on your door around six and we can head over."

Paula watched him leave and a moment later, Aunt Tessa walked in, looking seriously annoyed.

"What's wrong?" Her aunt was almost always in a good mood.

"I stopped across the street just now and talked to the manager, Marshall something or other. I told him I was rejecting his offer. He didn't even know what I was talking about! Can you imagine that? Said I have to call the corporate offices."

"That's okay. You can do it on Monday. Or just send them a letter back. I'm happy to help you write one, if you don't want to deal with it." Her aunt looked relieved at the suggestion.

"Could you? That would be great if you don't mind doing it. I have to admit, I'll be glad to not have to worry about this anymore. I think you'll be able to deal with these people better. I just want to get on my boat and sail away!"

Paula smiled and put a hand on her aunt's arm. "Why don't you have a seat and relax? Want a cup of tea? I was just about to have one."

"Oh, that sounds lovely. Tell Barbara to join us, too."

Paula went to make tea for the two of them while Barbara poured herself a coffee and started chatting with her aunt. Paula was glad that her aunt had so much faith in her ability to handle whatever might be coming her way with the new store opening soon. She was nervous, but hoped that she would make her proud.

CHAPTER 3

When Paula pulled into her driveway, she noticed that her neighbor, Hope, was sitting outside, with a sketchbook in her lap. She knew better than to interrupt while Hope was lost in her creative world, but Hope waved her over. Paula walked over and took a look at what she was working on. It was an incredibly realistic sketch of the cottages, the wildflowers and beach grass.

"That's really lovely."

Hope smiled as she packed up her pencils. "Thanks, the light was perfect today. I just finished a few minutes ago."

Paula leaned against the porch railing. "Do you have plans tonight? Our new neighbor, Quinn, invited me to go to the Surf Shack tonight."

"Oh? That sounds fun."

"Why don't you come with us? Unless you have plans?" Paula hoped that Hope was available. It would make the night out feel less like a date and more like friends grabbing a bite together if she went.

But Hope shook her head. "I told my brother I'd go to dinner with him and I think he has his heart set on Italian. Besides, you'll get to know Quinn better if it's just the two of you. You can report back to me with all the details."

"It's not a date," Paula said.

Hope laughed. "Okay. It's two people trying to figure out if they want to just be friends. He is cute."

"Hm. He's not planning to stick around here long, though."

"So what? You don't have to marry the guy. Just have dinner with him. Have fun."

"You're right. I think I'm just nervous because it's been a while since I've gone out with anyone, friend or otherwise."

Hope looked sympathetic. "How long has it been since you and Dan broke up?"

"Almost a year, if you can believe it." Almost a year since she'd ended her engagement with the guy she'd dated for six years. Dan was a software salesman, very successful, and he traveled constantly. When they went out they always had fun, but they'd grown apart as they saw each other less and less. It had been easy and comfortable but both of them felt the shift after Dan proposed.

Oddly enough, that was when they both pulled back some and realize that maybe they didn't want to spend the rest of their lives with each other. When

Paula broke things off, Dan admitted that he'd proposed because it seemed like the expected next step, not because he was madly in love and dying to marry her. Both of them knew that the passion just wasn't there.

"We both stayed in that relationship too long. It was too easy to keep it going the way it was," Paula said.

"And getting engaged was like a wake-up call?"

"Sort of. I know I wasn't as excited as I should have been. It was still sad when we ended it, though. We'd been in each other's lives for so long. But it was the right thing to do. I actually heard that he's pretty serious about someone that he works with now."

Hope looked surprised. "Oh? How do you feel about that?"

"I'm happy for him. And not jealous in the least. So, I guess we made the right call."

"So, go out and have fun. Even if there's no romantic spark, maybe he has a friend that will turn out to be 'the one'."

"That's a good point. Okay. I should get moving then. I need a hot shower."

Hope laughed. "You do. I see flour in your hair!" She folded up her sketchbook and picked up her box of pencils. "Keep me posted," she added.

"I will."

An hour later, Paula was showered and changed. Even though it wasn't a date, it still sort of felt like one, as she found herself having a hard time deciding what to wear. She finally settled on a pretty aqua top made of thin cotton and her favorite faded jeans. She used her curling iron to add a few beachy waves to her long, dark brown hair and slicked a bit of pink gloss across her lips. A little mascara and dusting of blush and she was ready.

The knock on the door came at six o'clock sharp. Paula opened the door and Quinn stood there looking very handsome. His blond hair was tousled in the breeze and he was already getting tanned. He was also wearing jeans and a blue plaid button-down shirt. His green eyes lit up when he saw her and when he smiled, a spray of tiny laugh lines appeared around his eyes and mouth. He looked like he laughed often and his eyes were warm and kind. Paula took a deep breath and relaxed a little.

"You look great," he said. "Are you ready to head out?"

"Thanks. I'm ready."

She grabbed her purse then followed him out and locked the door behind her. It was a warm night, with a light breeze, and there were still people coming off the beach. They walked along, chatting easily. The Surf Shack was only about a half a mile away and in about ten minutes, they reached the restaurant. Like most buildings in the greater Charleston area, it had huge, covered porches on the first and second floors.

They were seated on the first floor porch, by a railing that was draped with strands of tiny white lights shaped like sea shells.

The hostess handed them both menus, and they debated what to get for cocktails.

"Have you ever had a Pain Killer?" Quinn asked.

"That's one of the most popular drinks in Charleston. It's good, like a Pina Colada. I usually stick to wine, though."

Their waitress came by to get their drinks order.

"I'll have a glass of chardonnay," Paula said.

"And I'll take a draft beer, whatever local IPA you have."

They ordered dinner when their waitress returned with the drinks. Paula got the shrimp and grits, and Quinn ordered a cheeseburger.

From where they sat they could see the beach, and the sky turn pink as the sun began to set. It was a view that Paula never tired of and that Quinn seemed to appreciate.

"I could get used to this," he said.

"I know. I can't imagine living anywhere else. What's it like where you live?" All she knew was that he lived in Savannah, which was Charleston's sister city and also on the water.

"You've been to Savannah?"

She nodded.

"I live on one of the squares. A few years back, I bought an old house and subdivided it into four units.

I live in one and rent the others out. Two are year-round rentals and one is an Airbnb."

"Oh, that sounds like it was a fun project. Most of those old houses are so huge."

"They are and it was a lot of fun. I may do it again with another house if I can find the right property. The squares are pretty but they don't have views like this."

"Have you stayed in this area before?" Paula was curious how he happened to come to Indigo Bay on his own.

"No. I've been to Charleston, of course, but never to Indigo Bay. My grandmother knows Caroline of Sweet Caroline's and that's how I was referred to Dallas and his cottages."

Paula smiled. "I think Caroline knows everyone. She's been in Indigo Bay as long as I can remember."

When their food arrived, Quinn's burger looked good. Paula could see steam coming off her bowl of shrimp and grits so she let it cool a bit before taking a bite. It was one of her favorite dishes and was on the menu of just about every restaurant in from Indigo Bay to Savannah. She especially liked the Surf Shack's version, which was a mound of creamy, cheesy yellow grits, topped with plump shrimp, and a pink sauce made of cream, shrimp stock, tomato and a bit of wine. It was rich and delicious.

"So, I was surprised to see you in that bakery. Your main job is marketing, I think you said?" Quinn dunked a French fry in ketchup before taking a bite.

"It is. That's about to change soon, though." Since her aunt had filled Barbara in on her plans, Paula felt comfortable sharing her news. She was excited to talk about it. "My aunt is going to retire and I'm going to be taking over the business."

Quinn suddenly coughed and reached for his beer.

"Are you okay?" she asked. He looked like he was choking.

Quinn took a deep breath and then another swig of beer. "I'm fine. Something just went down wrong." He smiled. "So, that's exciting. It's a big change from marketing."

"It is. I've always worked part-time in the shop, though, and I really love it. And now I'll be able to try out some of my marketing ideas. My aunt was never big on that."

"Older people are often resistant to change," he agreed.

"What about you? What did you say you did?"

"It's not that exciting, really. I'm on the road a lot, overseeing training of new employees." He grinned and Paula felt a little shiver as his eyes met hers. His smile was dangerously charming. He picked up his burger. "I'm on vacation, though, for the next two weeks, so let's not talk about work any more, if that's all right with you?"

She laughed. "That is just fine with me. So, what do you plan to do while you're here relaxing?"

"I thought it might be kind of fun to play tourist. I

was thinking about heading into Charleston tomorrow and doing one of those walking tours, where they take you through the historic district, pointing out the architecture and different landmarks. Have you ever done that?"

"I haven't actually. I've heard good things about it, though."

"Why don't you come with me?" He leaned forward and his eyes took on a mischievous gleam. "We can play tourist together."

Paula had no plans for the next day, except for sleeping late and doing laundry to get ready for the week ahead.

"Sure. That sounds like fun."

When they finished eating, they both ordered another drink and after Quinn paid the bill, they went upstairs where there was a DJ setting up for karaoke.

"Do you sing?" Quinn asked as they found seats at a small cocktail table.

She laughed at the thought. "No, I'm completely tone deaf. It's very sad. Do you?"

"I've been known to get up there now and then. It depends on my mood and what the crowd is like."

Paula was intrigued. "What would you sing?"

"What would you like me to sing?"

"You'll sing anything I want?"

"Well, within reason of course. It depends on your taste in music."

She thought for a moment. "How about Tom Petty or Jimmy Buffett?"

He nodded. "Both excellent choices."

"So, you'll sing tonight?" She was looking forward to it and very curious to see how he'd do.

"We'll see. It's a strong maybe. Depends on how the night goes and if anyone shows up to sing."

"I've been here for karaoke before and there's usually a crowd of regulars that show up right before it starts. Once they begin, it draws a lot of people upstairs."

Sure enough, as they sat watching the sun set and enjoying the soft evening breeze, the upstairs bar began to fill up and once the DJ announced karaoke, the regulars appeared. People lined up to write their song choices on little slips of paper and hand them in. The first few people who got up to sing were terrible.

"So, are you going up?" Paula asked.

"I might as well, right? I can't be much worse than that." Quinn grinned and got up to submit a song slip. A few minutes later, he sat back down and Paula immediately asked what song he'd picked. But he refused to say.

"You'll see. It will spoil the surprise if I tell you now."

They listened to three more people sing, two who were pretty good, before Quinn's name was called.

"Good luck," she said as he headed to the mic.

The music began to play, and she laughed as she recognized the familiar song. Jimmy Buffett's Cheeseburger in Paradise. Quinn's voice was strong, and the song was a fun one for a bar. The crowd sang along and cheered when he finished.

They stayed for a few more songs and both of them laughed when Dallas showed up with some friends and was immediately recruited to join two girls who were on their way up to sing Love Shack. They all started singing together, but the girls took a step back and let Dallas do his thing. His voice was great and the lively song was a big hit with the crowd. By the end, everyone was singing along.

"That was amazing," Quinn said, when the song ended. "Are you about ready to head out? The walking tour is at ten tomorrow morning."

Paula followed Quinn out and they both stopped for a moment to say hello to Dallas, and to congratulate him on singing so well.

The sky was clear, and the air was still warm as they made their way home. Paula was intrigued by her new neighbor. He'd been friendly throughout dinner, and she'd enjoyed his company. She didn't get a strong romantic vibe from him, which was fine. She wasn't sure if she wanted to go there with anyone yet. But, especially since he lived right next door, she didn't want to rush anything. She was happy to keep it light and fun.

When they reached her cottage, he walked her to her door and then pulled her in for a good night hug.

"Thanks for coming out with me tonight. I had a great time," he said softly.

"I did, too. Thanks so much for dinner." Paula

had offered when the bill game, but Quinn wouldn't take her money.

"I'll come by around nine tomorrow. That should give us time to drive into Charleston and find parking before the tour starts."

"See you in the morning."

CHAPTER 4

When the phone rang at eight the next morning, Quinn knew who it was. No one else called him that early. He was sitting on his porch, enjoying his morning coffee and looking forward to the trip into town with Paula. He'd had a better time with her than he'd expected.

Paula was easy to talk to, smart, and fun. And of course, she was pretty, too. He'd been attracted to her when they first met and after spending time together, he found her even more intriguing and was looking forward to getting to know her even better.

He frowned, though, thinking of the one major issue standing between them. The one she didn't yet know about. He set his coffee on the small table beside him, reached for his cell phone, and smiled when he saw the familiar number.

"Good morning, Gram."

"I didn't wake you, did I?" She always asked that,

and it struck him funny. Like her, he was always up early, too.

"No, I'm up and out on my porch enjoying this sunny morning. It looks like it's going to be a good day."

"That's nice. Well, two things. I booked an appointment for you for next Friday at ten, your first day back to work. I'll email you the details, it's right in town and shouldn't take much time. I have another update for you, and it's not a good one." She sounded irritated. His grandmother was used to getting her own way.

"Tessa won't agree to sell," he said calmly.

"Yes, how did you know that?" He could hear the surprise in her voice.

"It's more complicated than we realized. Her niece lives next to me. We went for dinner and drinks last night and she told me that Tessa is retiring and she's taking over the business."

"Hmmm. What's she like, this Paula?"

"She's impressive. She's a few years younger than me, and works in marketing now. She seems excited to make a go of her aunt's shop."

"Oh, dear. She's not likely to last, once we open our doors. Maybe you can make her see reason. I'd prefer to buy her out, as you know."

"I know."

"Does she know who you are? I'm guessing probably not if she agreed to have dinner with you?"

"We're actually going on one of those walking

tours in Charleston today, too. And no, she doesn't know. I only just found out last night. Well, I knew her aunt owned the store, but not that she was taking over."

"Well, use your best judgment. See if you can charm her into doing what's best for everyone."

"We'll see." Quinn knew his grandmother meant well, but Quinn didn't want to charm Paula into doing anything, except spending more time with him. He was actually dreading telling her who he was and why he was in Indigo Bay. He didn't imagine there was any way that news would go over well.

AT NINE SHARP, he knocked on Paula's door and smiled when she opened it and he saw her. She looked cute in shorts and a long sleeved, pink top. Her hair was pulled back into a sleek ponytail, but a few stray pieces broke free and framed her face. She was even prettier in broad daylight than she'd been the night before, if that was possible. When she smiled, he felt all warm inside. He'd had plenty of crushes on gorgeous girls before, but something about this was different and he liked it, a lot.

"Good morning," she said as she stepped onto the porch.

"This should be fun. I'll need you to guide me once we get downtown," he said as they walked toward his Jeep. They climbed in and Paula directed him once they got into Charleston. It was a quick ride, just about a half hour with no traffic, and soon they were parking and walking over to the meeting spot for the tour. They were a few minutes early, so they decided to get coffees to enjoy as they walked.

Their tour guide, Scott, was an older man in his early sixties and he was full of enthusiasm. He checked their names off his list and once all twenty or so people were accounted, for he told them about the tour.

"We're going to spent the next two hours walking around the historic district and stopping at various points of interest. I'll also point out other houses and museums you might want to explore further on your own. Now, if everyone's ready, we're off!"

He led them a few blocks down the street before stopping in front of an old building that used to be a hotel and was now a theater. They went inside and everyone was impressed with the high ceilings, detailed carvings along the ceiling and doors and the rare rosewood of the doors themselves. It was a gorgeous building that had been lovingly restored.

As they walked along the streets, he pointed out architectural details of the houses they passed, explaining why so many of the large homes had porches that extended the full length of the home and were on every floor.

"The porches helped with cooling and heating of the homes, keeping the sun away and holding heat in during colder months."

They walked along the famous rainbow row where all the homes were different pastel colors and by the Old Slave Mart on Chalmers street. Now a museum, at one time it was where slaves were bought and sold. It was a sobering reminder of the dark side of Charleston's history.

By the time they finished the tour, it was after noon.

"Are you hungry?" Quinn was starving after all that walking.

"I am. There's a good restaurant right around the corner. They have the best she-crab soup."

"Lead the way."

Paula took him a few blocks down the street and stopped at 82 Queen, which was also the name of the restaurant. His stomach rumbled as the waiter led them to a table and he saw a tray of food come out of the kitchen. It smelled great.

Once they were seated, they both ordered sweet tea and she-crab soup. They shared an appetizer of fried green tomatoes topped with pimento cheese and Paula had a shrimp salad. He got the barbecued shrimp and grits.

The soup and appetizer arrived quickly, along with a basket of hot bread, and they both dug in.

"This soup always reminds me of my grandmother," he said.

"Oh? Is she a good cook?"

He laughed at that thought. "No. She doesn't

cook at all, but her housekeeper does. Marie made this soup a lot. Everything she made was good."

A cloud came over Paula's face. "You're lucky to still have your grandmother."

"I know. She's in her early eighties but you'd never know it. Still full of energy and sharp as a tack."

"She sounds wonderful. Does she live in Savannah, too?"

"She does. The whole family lives there. I have three brothers and a younger sister."

She looked at him with interest as if she was thinking about something. "I bet you're the oldest."

"I am, but how did you know?" He was curious.

"Just a lucky guess. You're very confident. Tell me about your family. Do your parents live there, too?"

He nodded. "They do. My father has a law practice and my mother doesn't work but is always busy. My sister thinks she wants to be an actress and my brothers are twins, actually, and both lawyers." He hesitated, as he didn't want the conversation to turn back to his work. He wasn't ready for his secret, or his brother Travis's, to come out just yet. They were having such a great day, so far. "Do you have any siblings?" He hoped to shift the conversation away from him.

She smiled as she spread a bit of pimento cheese on a piece of bread. "No, it's just me. I always wished I had a brother or sister, though, or both." She sounded wistful.

"Well, I can tell you that more than once I wished

that I was an only child. Siblings can be annoying. We get along pretty well now, though, for the most part."

After they finished eating, they walked around some more and decided to tour one of the old mansions. The Nathanial Russell house was a grand house that had been built by a wealthy shipping merchant, sold to a governor, and was now a historic landmark and tourist attraction.

"Can you imagine living in a house this big?" Paula asked as they made their way up the elaborate spiral staircase to the second floor.

Quinn looked around the grand hall and the elegant rooms with their high ceilings. "No, I can't imagine it. It's not my style at all."

"It's lovely, but I think it would be strange to have a houseful of servants. I much prefer my cozy cottage."

"I'm pretty happy with mine, too." Quinn thought of his immaculate condo in Savannah. It was a little bigger than his cottage in Indigo Bay, but the cottage, with its simple furnishings, was comfortable and more inviting than his cold condo. If he didn't travel so much, he might see about hiring someone to make his place feel more homey.

On the ride home, Paula asked him what else he planned to do while on vacation.

"I'm playing it by ear. Doing whatever I feel like doing. It's a nice change. I think I might do a little fishing when we get home. I hear that it's pretty good off the pier." There was a long pier not too far down the beach and he'd been meaning to try his luck once he heard it was a good spot.

"Do you love to fish? I haven't done it since I as a kid."

"It's been a year or so for me, but I love to do it when I get a chance. It's relaxing. And I always eat what I catch. Why don't you come along?"

"I'd actually love to, but I can't today. I'm heading to my parents for Sunday dinner. Another time, maybe?"

"Sure thing. Anytime you feel like it, just let me know." He pulled up to his cottage and parked. "Thanks for coming today. I'm glad we did that," he said as they walked along the sand toward the cottages.

"I am, too. Thanks for inviting me. Good luck fishing." Paula smiled as she headed off to her cottage. Quinn stepped onto his porch and watched until she was inside. It had been a good day. He was eager to spend more time with his new neighbor but dreading the day she found out who he was.

AS SHE DID every Sunday afternoon, Paula did a load of laundry for the week ahead. She put her clothes in the dryer before she left and ten minutes, later pulled into her parent's driveway. Her contribution for the dinner was a salted caramel coffee cake she'd made early that morning. It was a new recipe she wanted to try for the shop and wanted to run it by her aunt first, to make sure she liked it.

Her parents and aunt were all sitting on the porch, sipping iced tea and snacking on a bowl of potato chips, when she arrived. Her mother's eyes lit up when she saw the cake Paula was holding.

"Oh, honey, that looks delicious. Set it in the kitchen and then come join us. There's a pitcher of fresh tea and a bottle of white wine if you'd rather have that."

Paula put the cake on the counter, poured herself a glass of ice water and brought it out to the porch. She settled into an empty rocking chair and automatically reached for a potato chip. She wasn't really hungry, but they were sitting right in front of her.

"So, are you going to tell us about your date?" Aunt Tessa looked at her eagerly and Paula cringed when she saw her mother and father both leaning forward in their chairs. She looked at her aunt in confusion.

"If you mean dinner with my new neighbor last night, it wasn't a date. How did you know about that, anyway?" The only person Paula had mentioned it to was Hope.

"I had breakfast at Sweet Caroline's this morning," Aunt Tessa said. "Sat at the counter next to her son, Dallas. He mentioned that he saw you at the Surf Shack. To be fair, he didn't say it was a date, either, just that he saw you there."

"Who is this young man? And why don't you want to date him?" her father asked.

"Yes, why don't you want to?" her mother chimed in.

Paula sighed. "He's very nice and I actually wouldn't mind dating him but I don't know if he's interested and more importantly, he's just passing through. He's here on vacation. He'll be gone in a few weeks."

"Well, where does he live? Maybe it's not too far." Her mother sounded hopeful.

"Savannah."

"Well, heck, that's Charleston's sister city, barely two hours away. That's nothing," her father said as he reached for the bowl of chips.

Paula smiled. She knew they meant well. "It's not just that. He travels a lot for his job. He's gone for weeks at a time."

"Oh, that's too bad. You're right honey, that probably wouldn't work at all," her mother agreed.

"What does he does he do for work?" Aunt Tessa wasn't ready to give up yet.

Paula realized that she knew very little about what Quinn did. "I'm not exactly sure. Something to do with the family business."

"Which is what?" her father asked.

Paula laughed. "I don't know. It didn't come up. He's on vacation, so said he didn't want to think about work for the next few weeks, so I didn't ask."

"Well, that's too bad." Her mother sounded disappointed. "I was excited thinking that you were out there dating again. It's been a while."

"It has," Paula agreed. And it had been nice to spend an evening with a nice, handsome man. Whether it was an actual date or not.

"Speaking of business," her aunt began. "I got a call from the head of Bakey's. She got my letter. We had a good conversation, but I let her know in no uncertain terms that I wouldn't be selling. And I told her that you're taking over soon. I don't think she was happy with my news."

"Are you sure you don't want to take her up on her offer? That's a lot of money to turn down." Her mother looked concerned.

But Aunt Tessa laughed. "Nonsense! I have plenty of money in the bank. And I'll be able to draw on my retirement account now, too. Besides, I'm leaving the shop in the very best hands. I have all the faith in the world that Paula is going to do a splendid job!"

Her mother smiled. "Well, of course she will. And I can't believe we're going to be leaving for that cruise in just a few weeks."

"You're both going to have a wonderful time on that trip. I'm a little jealous." Paula laughed, picturing the two of them roaming around the giant ship. She knew they were going to have a ball.

"You'll be too busy to give it much thought," Aunt Tessa said with a wicked grin.

"It's going to be quiet around here," her father said.

"I'll come visit you while they're gone," Paula assured him.

"Oh, I'm not complaining. I'm looking forward to the peace and quiet." He winked at her mother and she slapped him on the arm, laughing. Paula watched her parents and how they still liked to tease each other. She knew they'd miss each other, yet they both were fine being apart ,too. Her father knew it was just for a few weeks and she had no doubt he'd find plenty to occupy his time while she was gone.

He had a circle of friends he often played cards and fished with, and saw nearly every day for breakfast at Sweet Caroline's. He was also a big reader, and she guessed he had a lineup of books he was eager to plow through. But still, she planned to invite him over for dinner and to visit him more than usual while her mother and aunt were away.

"Have you given your notice at work yet?" Aunt Tessa asked her as they went inside to sit down for dinner.

"No, not yet. I'll do that sometime this week. I want to give them notice, of course, but not too far ahead of time, just in case they decide they don't want me to stay on."

"They wouldn't do that, would they?" Her mother seemed shocked at the idea. But Paula had seen it happen before, particularly with sales people. Since she was in marketing and client management, she didn't expect to be let go immediately, but she still thought it was safer to be cautious, just in case.

“They probably won’t do that to me. We’re a bit short-handed at the moment, so I think they’ll appreciate having me there to transition someone onto my accounts.”

“Good. Now, everyone grab a plate and come into the kitchen to help yourselves.”

CHAPTER 5

Paula's week flew by. She was a little tired when she went into work on Friday and was planning to put her two-week notice in. They'd all gone out the night before—Hope, Von, Quinn and Dallas for Taco Thursday and Team Trivia at the Surf Shack. Hope and Paula occasionally went on Thursdays. The fish and shrimp tacos were fantastic, and they both liked playing trivia.

It was definitely more fun with a larger group, though, and they all had their topics they were good at. For Hope and Paula it was entertainment and news and the guys generally knew the sports and history questions. Quinn fit in easily with their small group of friends and everyone seemed to like him. Hope shared her concerns about getting too close to him, given his temporary status and heavy travel.

But still, Paula saw him several times during the week. Monday night, he'd knocked on her door with the cutest expression. He'd caught a bunch of fish, more than he could eat, and wondered if she was hungry? As soon as he asked, she could smell the tantalizing scent of the fresh fish wafting over from his grill and she happily joined him on his porch for dinner.

On Wednesday night, she returned the favor by having him and Hope over for dinner at her place. She'd made a pot of meatballs and sauce in her slow cooker that morning and it was ready when she got home. And then they all went to trivia Thursday night. She was getting used to hanging out with him and realized she was going to miss him when he left.

Paula noticed a buzz in the air when she walked into the office a little before nine. She made herself a cup of coffee, settled in at her desk and began to check her email. The agency was small, with only about twenty employees, but they were growing and building a strong reputation in Charleston for their digital marketing results. Paula was one of five account managers that handled marketing strategy and client contact for their bigger clients.

The other senior level account manager was Naomi Tolliver, and she was one person Paula would not miss. Naomi grated on her last nerve. She was an ex-Miss Charleston and still seemed to be competing for the title with the way she dressed and acted. She was always sucking up to the agency owner and seeking approval and attention. She was slim and curvy with long, platinum blonde curls, big blue eyes and an annoyingly high-pitched voice.

Naomi looked up from her desk, which was so clean it almost looked like no one used it, and smiled her sickly sweet smile when she saw Paula. "Well, don't you look like something the cat dragged in? Late night last night? Hope it was fun!"

Paula frowned and pulled a compact mirror out of her purse. She looked a little tired, but Naomi made it sound so much worse. Still, she slicked on a bit of pink lipstick to brighten her look, and dabbed a little powder under her eyes to hide the slight circles.

A moment later, Maxine, the stylish, sixty-something woman that owned the agency, strolled into the room and everyone turned her way. Maxine usually stayed in her glass-walled corner office and only came into the main room where all the employees sat when there was something to announce. As soon as she had everyone's attention, she spoke.

"I have exciting news. We have a big new client coming in to meet with us at ten. Paula, I'll want you to take the lead on this, but Naomi I want you in the meeting, too, as this could turn into a national account."

"Who's the client?" Naomi asked.

Maxine smiled. "Bakey's. They're opening a new store in Indigo Bay and they want us to help with the opening and building brand awareness locally. If we do a good job, they may tap us to help as they roll out new locations across the country. It's a huge opportunity for us!"

Paula's heart sank. She waited until Maxine went back to her office, and then she followed her and knocked softly on her door. She'd originally planned to give her notice at the end of the day, but that timeline needed to be moved up, ASAP.

"Oh, hello, Paula. Come on in. Are you as excited about this new account as I am?"

Paula chose her words carefully. "It's very exciting and a great opportunity for the agency."

Maxine nodded and looked pleased to hear it.

"I'm afraid it's not the best timing, though. I think you may want to have Naomi take the lead on this one."

Maxine frowned. "Oh? I thought this would be a great fit for you. You're such a foodie and you still help your aunt at her bakery sometimes, don't you?"

Paula nodded. "I do, and that's actually what I need to talk to you about. I'm afraid there's a conflict of interest. My aunt is retiring and I'm going to take over the business. I've loved working here, but I was actually planning to give my two weeks notice today."

"Oh, my goodness!" Maxine looked shocked. She took a moment to digest the news and then sighed. "Well, I'm happy for you, of course. And I agree, it doesn't make sense for you to meet with the client now. We'll have Naomi go in your place. And maybe for the next two weeks, you can help her and transition a few of your clients over to her."

She peered over her glasses at Paula and squinted as if she was trying to focus her thoughts. "Are you sure about this? You've done very well here. You could have a long career in marketing."

Paula smiled. Maxine had been a wonderful mentor, but she knew in her heart it was time to move on. "I am sure. I'm going to miss everyone here, but I'm excited about this next step."

Maxine took a deep breath. "All right, then. I'm excited for you, too. Can you please send Naomi in here? I'll need to give her the good news."

A half hour later, Naomi came bouncing back to her desk, with a satisfied smile on her face. "Maxine told me your news. I'm sorry to see you go, of course. You're really going to run a bakery? Instead of work in marketing?" The look of distaste on her face was comical. Clearly, Naomi avoided doing anything in the kitchen.

"I love cooking and baking. It's deeply satisfying and relaxing, too. And I'm looking forward to the challenge of running a business."

Naomi frowned. "Aren't you a little worried, though, about Bakey's opening up? Their location is near yours, I think?"

"Right across the street," Paula confirmed. "We'll be fine. We have a strong client base. I'm sure they did their research and determined that there's enough business here to support both of us."

"They do seem to know what they're doing. And the person we're meeting with is hot. He's the grandson of the CEO." She did a quick internet search and then added, "And it looks like he's about our age, and single. I am looking forward to meeting Quinn Jacobs."

Paula dropped her pen. "What did you say his name is?"

"Quinn Jacobs. Oh, it looks like he's here now. Amy just buzzed me that he's in the lobby. See you later." She ran off to get Maxine while Paula sat there in shock. How had she not put it together before? Quinn had mentioned working for the family business, and he knew what she was doing. Was it also his idea to use the marketing firm she worked at, too? And why hadn't he told her who he was? Paula felt like an idiot. An angry one.

She got up and walked into the lobby, determined to see for herself that Quinn was sitting there. Maxine and Naomi were shaking his hand and about to lead him into the conference room when he saw her and his jaw dropped.

"Paula."

"Hello, Quinn. I see your vacation is over?"

He had the grace to flush before flashing what she used to think was a charming smile. "Back to work today. My grandmother set this meeting up. I didn't know you worked here."

She smiled sweetly, but it didn't reach her eyes and there was an edge to her voice as she said, "And I didn't know you worked at Bakey's."

Naomi and Maxine both looked confused. "You two know each other?" Naomi asked.

"Paula nodded. "Quinn is renting the cottage next to me." She glanced at Quinn. "You're in good hands with these two." She turned and walked back to her desk, still furious that he hadn't told her who he was, but glad that at least he hadn't known she worked at the agency.

She made herself another cup of coffee and tried to focus on her work. Her anger gradually faded and was replaced by a keen sense of disappointment. She'd liked Quinn and thought they were friends. She'd even flirted with the possibility of imagining something more, but that hope was permanently dashed now.

QUINN WATCHED as Paula walked away and his heart sank. She was the last person he'd want to be upset with him. She was smiling when she spoke to him but he'd heard the hurt and coldness in her voice. This wasn't how he wanted her to find out. He'd planned to tell her before he went back to work, but the timing hadn't been right. He'd never wanted to ruin the mood. And now it was shattered.

"Quinn, if you could follow us into the conference room? I think you'll be excited by what we have in mind for you!" Naomi, the bubbly blonde was smiling at him.

"Sure, of course." He followed the two women into the conference room where there was a tray of pastries and a carafe of coffee waiting.

"Would you like coffee?" Naomi offered.

He couldn't care less about coffee, but since they'd gone to some trouble for him, he agreed to a cup and selected a cheese danish as well. Once they all had coffee, Maxine and Naomi ran through what they had in mind for Facebook and other web marketing to support the opening of the store. He wasn't any kind of marketing expert, so it all sounded good to him.

When he finished his pastry, he couldn't help but smile at the name of the bakery on the napkin, The Sweet Shop, Paula's aunt's place. That was ironic, considering. Maxine noticed his gaze and smiled.

"I hope you don't mind. If there was a Bakey's in the area, of course we would have gotten them there."

"No worries, it's fine. They're delicious, actually."

"So, Naomi will be your contact person and she'll be on site as well for your grand opening party. We'll really make a nice event of it."

"That sounds great. This is all Greek to me, but my grandmother said you ladies are the best in town."

Maxine looked pleased to hear it. "Your grandmother and I go way back. Will she be coming to the opening party? I'd love to see her."

Quinn doubted it. His grandmother rarely left Savannah, but since Charleston wasn't that far, it was a possibility. "I don't know. She hasn't mentioned it, but maybe she will."

"Will you be staying in Charleston long?" Naomi asked and by the way she batted her eyelashes and leaned forward, he sensed her interest. But Naomi, with her pouffy white-blonde hair and perfectly manicured nails, was not his type, at all. He preferred ponytails and hands with short nails so they could work better with pastry dough.

"I'm not sure. I'm only supposed to be here for a few weeks, to get the store up and running."

"Right. Well, here's my card. Call me anytime…if you have any questions about anything at all." She smiled again as he took the card and slid it into his pocket. He hoped that he wouldn't need to call.

He stopped at the new store when he left the agency and was impressed with what he saw. Marshall, the general manager, had everything well under control and he was already training new employees in the kitchen. He stayed an hour but there wasn't much for him to do there. His laptop was at the cottage and he could get more done there, fielding all the emails that came in on a regular basis.

When he got home, instead of breaking for lunch, he decided to go for a run on the beach. He was still full from the mid-morning pastry and he needed to burn off some nervous energy. An hour later, he walked back to the cottage, rinsed off in the outside shower and settled in the kitchen on his laptop for the rest of the afternoon.

He was anxious for Paula to get home, to talk to her and to see if he could make things right, somehow. A little after five, he heard the familiar sound of her car as it pulled into her driveway. He wanted to walk over there and see her in person, but he knew she might not want that.

So, he waited about ten minutes and then called her to see if they could talk. She didn't pick up, so he left her a message. He knew she was inside. When fifteen minutes went by and she didn't call him back, he had a feeling that he wasn't going to hear from her that night, anyway.

He took his laptop out to his porch and thought about what to do for dinner. There was no food in his house, so he either had to go to the grocery store or go out to eat. Maybe he'd just walk to the Surf Shack in a while and grab a bite to eat at the bar. He was feeling a little stir crazy, and a beer and a burger sounded pretty good.

"Meow…" Quinn heard the cry as he felt something soft and furry brush against his leg. He looked down and saw a fluffy orange cat looking up at him. "Meow…." It rubbed its head against his calf and then cocked its head expectantly.

Quinn laughed. "Well, hello there." He reached over and scratched the cat behind its ears. Loud purring commenced, so he kept scratching and patting. A moment later, the cat jumped into his lap and walked around, meowing loudly.

"Who are you?" he asked the cat as he continued to pet it. The cat walked in circles and then flopped down and started washing its paw, while still purring.

"Where did you come from?" he asked as he took a good look at the little cat. There was a lot of fur but underneath, the cat was tiny, bony even. "Are you hungry? Do you want some food?"

At the word 'food' the cat jumped up and started rubbing its head against his hand.

"Okay, hold on. Let me go see what I've got." He went inside and found a can of tuna in a cabinet. He opened it and dumped it onto a paper plate, then brought it outside and set it down for the cat. The cats tail twitched as it gobbled down the tuna. It disappeared in a flash. Quinn set down a dish of water, too, but the cat was less excited about that. When it was done eating, it jumped back into his lap and began giving itself a bath. That's when Quinn noticed the cat was a she.

The little cat purred as she washed herself and then curled up and closed her eyes. She slept on Quinn's lap for about an hour before stretching lazily and then wandering off toward the beach. He wondered if he'd see her again. He guessed she probably lived nearby. She was a cute little thing, and he'd been glad for the company. He picked up his phone and saw that there was still no text or voice messages.

He'd noticed a pizza delivery guy going to Paula's door a little while ago and heard laughter as one of her kitchen windows was open. He guessed that Hope was sharing the pizza with her. He'd thought about going out to dinner but now he was feeling lazy and ordering a pizza sounded like a good idea. He'd do that and go see what was on TV—and try not to think about Paula.

~

PAULA HAD CALLED Hope on the way home from work and asked if she had dinner plans.

"No, I was going to read a book or see what was on Netflix. Exciting Friday night, huh? Do you have a better idea?"

"Yes. Come over. We can order a pizza and have ice cream. I have two pints of Ben and Jerry's Salted Carmel Swirl in the freezer."

"Your secret stash! Are you okay?" Hope knew that ice cream was for emergencies only.

"I'm fine. Or I will be. Just disappointed. I'll fill you in when you come over."

"Okay, I'll see you at six?"

"Perfect."

Paula had noticed that Quinn's car was in his driveway when she pulled up. He must have heard her car as well because five minutes after she walked through the door, her cell phone rang and it was him. She let the call go to voice mail, though. She was still too angry and disappointed to talk to him. As soon as her phone flashed that he'd left a message, she hit play to listen to it.

"Paula, it's Quinn. I really want to talk to you." He paused for a moment. "I'm so sorry. I wanted to tell you myself. I certainly didn't expect you to find out like that. I hope we can still....be friends. Call me."

She shook her head and then turned at the sound of steps on the porch. It was Hope.

"Come on in."

Paula set a takeout pizza menu on the kitchen table and got two tall glasses out of a cabinet, filled both with ice and then poured lemonade into both. She added a pinch of fresh mint and straws, and handed one to Hope who'd settled at the kitchen table and was studying the pizza options.

"Thanks. Do you want to get the usual?" The usual was a large pizza with spinach, feta, thin fried eggplant slices, and mozzarella.

"Yes, and a side of fried zucchini."

While they waited for the pizza, Paula filled Hope in on her day. She shook her head and looked as disappointed as Paula felt.

"That stinks. I'm really sorry. I liked Quinn. I thought...well, it doesn't matter what I thought. I guess you just don't know people, huh?"

"No. As if I needed the reminder. I guess the old saying is true. If something seems too good to be true, it probably is." Paula reached for a can of salted, mixed nuts that was in the middle of the kitchen table where they were sitting.

"Want some nuts? I'm starving." She reached for a handful and crunched on a salted pecan.

"Sure, why not?" Hope said and Paula pushed the can toward her.

"He left me a message just before you got here. He sounded apologetic and said he hopes we can be friends."

Hope frowned. "Do you think you can? He's only here for a few more weeks, right?"

"Right. Just until the new store is up and running. That's what he does, evidently. Goes around the country opening new locations."

"Well, I do sort of understand why he didn't tell you. It's kind of an awkward thing to bring up once he found out you were taking over your aunt's shop."

"True, but still. It had to come out eventually." That's what annoyed Paula the most, that he hadn't broken the news himself.

"And he may have been planning to tell you soon. You said he had no idea you worked at that agency? His grandmother set it up?"

"That's what he said. And what if they do kill our business? That's something my aunt didn't even want to deal with and while I hope it won't come to that, it is a possibility. It's happened in other locations when they've opened."

"It won't happen with you." Hope sounded confident and Paula loved her for it. "This is your chance to put those marketing ideas into action. I know you'll do great."

"Thank you." She took a deep breath. "I hope so."

CHAPTER 6

Paula went to bed early, not long after Hope went home. She'd stayed for pizza and ice cream, and they'd watched a romantic comedy on the Hallmark Channel which fit their moods perfectly. It was about nine when she climbed into bed. As tired as she was, she noticed that Quinn had stayed in, too. The light in his living room was still on when she went to sleep. She'd thought about calling him back after Hope left, but it still felt too soon.

She arrived at The Sweet Shop at six a.m. sharp the next day. Barbara was already there and was mixing up a huge batch of dough to make donuts. When their doors opened, those were the first thing most people wanted, along with coffee.

Paula was glad to get busy. She had two wedding cakes to decorate, which always put her in a good mood. She'd noticed when she parked that workers were already across the street as well. She still couldn't see in as all the windows were covered with brown paper, but she could see the glow of lights peeking out. There was a big sign out front with the Bakey's logo that said they were opening two weeks from Monday. On the day she was officially taking over the shop.

Bakey's was at least three times the size of their store. She knew that they usually did a big commercial business, supplying bread to local area restaurants. Her aunt had never gone after that business, so she didn't feel like they were missing out. The Sweet Shop focused on cakes, muffins and other pastries. They sold loaves of bread, too, but it wasn't a big seller for them.

Which was fine with Paula. If she did nothing but make cakes and decorate them, she'd be happy. And running the business, too, of course. She was excited to get started with some of her marketing ideas. As soon as her aunt officially retired, which was in a little less than two weeks. Her last day was going to be the Thursday before Paula started, and their cruise left on Saturday. Aunt Tessa was getting out just before Bakey's opened.

"It's going to be strange around here without your aunt," Barbara said as she dropped a batch of donuts into the deep fryer.

"I know. Maybe she'll miss it and want to work part-time," Paula said. She knew that Barbara would love that. She and her aunt had a strong friendship and had worked together for nearly ten years. Paula hoped that she might want to come back part-time, too, as much or as little as she wanted.

It was a busy day, as Saturdays always were. It finally slowed around two and by a quarter to three, the shop was nearly empty. Paula was almost done wrapping everything up when the front door chimed and a familiar face walked in. Quinn walked up to the counter and Paula froze, waiting for him to speak.

"Hi."

"Hi, Quinn."

He ran a hand through his hair and seemed a little nervous. "I'm sorry to bother you here, but I tried to reach you last night. I didn't want to just knock on your door. I left a voice message."

Paula nodded. "I got it. I was busy last night. Hope came over for dinner. We had some pizza."

"Yeah, I saw the delivery truck." He smiled. "It made me want pizza, too. I ended up ordering from the same place."

"What do you want, Quinn? Can I get you something?" Paula was both annoyed and intrigued that Quinn came into the store.

"I'll take two cannoli, but I really wanted to just see you and apologize in person. I should have told you sooner about Bakey's and my connection to it. I was planning on it. I just kept waiting for the right time and chickening out. But, I had no idea the marketing agency I had an appointment with was the one you worked at."

"I know. I could tell. You looked almost as surprised as I was." Paula rang him up and handed him a paper bag with the cannoli in it.

"Thanks. What are you up to later? Can I take you out for an apology dinner?"

She shook her head. "You don't have to do that. To be honest, I'm exhausted. I don't think I'm up for going out anywhere."

"Okay, how about Plan B?"

"What's that?"

"Leftover pizza, and cannoli at my place. We can hang out and watch movies. You can go home whenever you're tired."

"I don't know." She was torn because part of her wanted to go and just have an enjoyable night, but she was still upset and needed to process who he was, and really talk to him about what this meant for The Sweet Shop.

Quinn flashed his most charming smile. "I'll even let you pick out the movie. Just come over whenever you get hungry."

She sighed, and finally gave in. "All right. I'll come, but I'm not sure how long I'll stay. But, I do need to talk to you more seriously about this."

He nodded. "I want that too. I'll see you in a little bit then." Quinn left. Paula watched him go and then locked the front door behind him. It was time to clean up and go home.

"Who was that?" Barbara asked. She was done cleaning up in the back and was ready to leave.

"That's my next-door neighbor, Quinn."

"Handsome. And he's interested in you."

"I don't know about that." Paula wasn't sure what to think. Knowing who Quinn was made everything more complicated. Plus, he didn't have any reason to stay in Indigo Bay any longer than he needed to. Savannah and the rest of the country was waiting for him.

"I know what I see. Anyway, I'm off. See you next Saturday."

"Bye, Barbara."

PAULA MADE a deposit at the bank on her way home and hopped in the shower as soon as she walked in the door. Her clothes stunk of sugar and butter and she had bits of flour in her hair. The hot water felt wonderful as it washed over her. Once she was changed and her long hair blown dry and pulled into a ponytail, she flopped on her living room sofa and read a magazine for a while. It was nice to just relax until it was time to go next door to Quinn's cottage. She was both looking forward to it and dreading the conversation at the same time.

At a few minutes past six, she knocked on his door. He opened it immediately, and she took a step back in surprise when she saw a fluffy orange cat doing figure eights around his legs.

"Who's that?"

He grinned. "My new best friend. I'm calling her Mary for now. She came by yesterday, meowing. I gave her some tuna and now she's back for more."

"She's cute. I've never seen her around here before."

"I hadn't either. But, she was so hungry yesterday that I had a feeling she might come visit again. I picked up some actual cat food when I was out earlier, too, just in case. I was just about to give it to her."

Paula stepped inside and watched as Quinn opened a can of food and dumped it on a paper plate. He set it on the floor and the little cat scampered over and started devouring it.

"I guess she likes it." Quinn smiled as he watched the cat attack the food. "What about you? Are you hungry?"

"I'm starving, actually." She'd been too busy at the shop to stop for lunch. "I brought some wine." She handed him a bottle of merlot.

"Oh, great. Thanks. I have plenty of leftover pizza we can heat up and a bag of salad."

"Okay."

"Do you want to open the wine while I mix the salad?"

Paula found his wine opener, then opened and poured wine for both of them.

"Do you want to sit outside on the porch? It's a beautiful night. We can talk a little before we eat?" Did she imagine that he sounded a bit nervous too?

Paula brought their wine outside and they sat on a

loveseat-sized rocking sofa, similar to the one on her porch. Mary, the cat, followed them outside and jumped up between them. She sprawled out and began to purr. Paula automatically reached over and scratched her behind her ears.

"Are you a cat person?" Quinn asked.

"Yes, we always had them growing up. I had one myself until a few months ago." Paula felt her eyes grow misty as she thought of the sweet cat she'd had for so many years. The house still felt empty without him. "Teddie was fourteen and had a long, happy life. I still miss him. I'll get another cat, eventually. I'm just not ready yet. What about you?"

"I love them. If I didn't travel so much, I'd definitely have at least one. But with my schedule, it's impossible."

And that brought her back to the conversation she needed to have.

"Quinn, I've really liked spending time with you. But you have to understand how hard this is for me now. Especially since I had no idea who you were."

He nodded. "I know. And I'm so sorry. The last thing I expected was to meet someone I'd care about while I was here on vacation. And then when you told me you were taking over your Aunt's shop, at the Surf Shack, well, I almost choked on my beer."

Paula smiled, remembering. "I thought something had just gone down wrong."

"We were having such a nice night. I didn't want to ruin the moment. I've wanted to tell you. But I've wanted to spend time with you more. I'm sorry, that I didn't though."

"So, I guess my question to you is, what does this mean for my shop? Part of the reason Aunt Tessa had me take over is because she didn't want to deal with it. At her age, she's not up for a fight and she wasn't ready to just hand her company over—even if the price was right. She's proud of that shop. She started it years ago, when she was about my age actually. She knows almost all her customers by name and they're very loyal to her. This was hugely upsetting. And as excited as I am to take this challenge on, I know the history of what has happened when Bakey's has opened in other areas. How can I date someone who might put us out of business?"

"I'm not going to let that happen," Quinn assured her.

Paula smiled sadly. "That's sweet, but how can you say that?"

"Hold on a sec. I want to show you something." Quinn stood up and went inside for a moment. He came back with an iPad and sat back down and started pulling something up.

"I've been working on the Bakey's menu and I think you might find it interesting."

He held the iPad so she could see the screen. Paula read through the list of bakery items, most of them pretty standard, but she was surprised when she saw the two bottom items, cannoli and wedding cakes, had a line struck through them.

"What does this mean?" she asked. Wedding cakes were a huge part of The Sweet Shop's business and it was what Paula enjoyed the most.

"It means that your cannoli are the best I've ever had, and I expect you're known for them?"

Paula nodded. "We are actually."

"So, I decided that we don't need to offer them. The same with wedding cakes. They're time intensive for one thing, but also it occurred to me, that it might be more beneficial for us to work together. If people want cannoli we can send them your way, same with wedding cakes. Then maybe we can support each other instead of competing so much."

Paula was stunned. "Your grandmother agreed to this?"

Quinn was quiet for a moment. "Not exactly. I haven't told her yet. We're talking in the morning. But she has given me the authority to decide store menus, based on what I see in the community, and that's my decision."

Paula was impressed, and felt her heart melting. She didn't expect anything Quinn to do anything like this.

"So, tell me more about what you do with the company. Have you worked there long?"

"I've been there since I got my MBA. I worked in a different industry entirely, for a software company, before I went to graduate school. I always knew I'd join Bakey's but my grandmother wanted me to work somewhere else for a few years, in a different industry, before getting my MBA. I thought it was a strange request at the time, but I've come to realize that she was right. It was good to have that experience." He smiled, and added, "She's almost always right."

"Do you work closely with her?'

"I do. I suppose you could say I'm her right-hand man. I travel a lot, to all the new locations as we open them and I manage that process from a higher level, trouble-shooting any issues that might come up." She could tell by the way he spoke that he enjoyed the work, and that he and his grandmother were close as well.

"Do you enjoy traveling that much? I don't think that I would."

"It can be a little tiring at times, but overall, I don't really mind it. I guess I'm used to it."

"Where are you off to after Indigo Bay?"

"Our next opening is in Kansas City. I'd like to stay here a few weeks longer, though. It's my first time living at the beach and I'm not ready to give it up yet."

"I can't imagine living anywhere else. I'd miss the beach too much. And my family, too, of course."

"That's what's kept me in Savannah. My family, and the business is headquartered there, too."

"Do you go into the office there much?"

"No, not really. I have an office there, but I'm usually on the road. All I really need is my laptop and my office can be anywhere."

When the food was ready, they filled their plates

with pizza and salad and settled on the porch to eat. Mary slept soundly between them as they ate and enjoyed the warm breezes blowing off the ocean.

"Is there a lot of work involved with a store opening?" Paula asked as she reached for her last bite of pizza.

"There is, but we have it down to a science now. As long as we have a good general manager on site, my role is mostly making sure they have everything they need to succeed. So, it's meeting with local marketing people sometimes or just overseeing things from a high level. I don't need to spend as much time with each store as I used to."

"Oh, that's good. So, you might not have to travel as much?"

He nodded. "I'm able to do more of the work remotely, so I will eventually be able to cut back some on the travel." He glanced at Mary. "Not enough to get a pet, though, unfortunately."

"You're liking having her around!"

"I am. She was good company the other night when I was waiting for a phone call that didn't come." He smiled charmingly and Paula chuckled.

"So what movie are we watching?" She changed the subject.

"You pick. I have Netflix. Are you ready for dessert?"

"I'm too full right now. Maybe later?"

He took her empty plate, and she followed him

inside. A moment later, Mary was outside the door meowing and Quinn let her inside as well.

They settled in the living room on a comfy sofa covered in a sturdy cream-colored canvas slip-cover. The shabby chic look was practical and perfect for a beach rental cottage. They sat on opposite sites of the sofa, and Mary hopped up behind them and sprawled out between them, looking down from her perch until they both petted her. A few minutes later, still purring, she fell fast asleep.

Paula flipped through the movie listings for romantic comedies and when she landed on When Harry Met Sally, Quinn admitted that he'd never seen it.

"It's a classic, and it's funny. Billy Crystal and Meg Ryan are both great. I've seen it a few times, but would love to introduce you to it, if you're up for it."

"Sure, let's see what all the fuss is about."

They spent the next two hours laughing. When the credits finally rolled, Quinn stood up and stretched. "You're right, that was a great film. So, are you ready for dessert now?"

Paula stood, too, and followed him to the kitchen. "Sure, but I should get going afterward. I'm starting to fade a little." Getting up so early was catching up with her.

"It's still nice out. We can have these on the porch and then I'll walk you home."

Paula smiled. "You don't have to walk me home. I'm right next door."

"Even so. It's late, and I'm a gentleman." He carried their desserts outside, and Mary ran out as well and disappeared in the dunes.

"I wonder where she goes," Paula said.

"I hope she'll be okay when I leave. I think she might be a stray."

"Well, I'll keep an eye out for her after you leave. She won't go hungry."

The cannoli was delicious, as Paula knew it would be. She'd made it earlier in the day and it was one of her favorite desserts. She loved the rich and creamy ricotta cheese filling and the delicate cookie shell. She took her last bit and then yawned. It was time to go.

"Hold on. I'll toss these plates in the trash and then walk you home." He returned a moment later and they both stepped off his porch, walked across the sand to hers and a minute later were at her door.

"Well, thank you for dinner and dessert. It was a perfect, relaxing night. And I'm glad you finally got to experience When Harry Met Sally." She grinned. "I don't know if I mentioned it earlier, but it's one of my all-time favorite movies. I've actually lost count of how many times I've seen it."

Quinn surprised her by taking hold of her hands and pulled her towards him.

"I've wanted to do this since the day I met you." His voice was husky as he leaned in and brought his lips to hers. She'd wanted it, too, even though she knew it was probably a bad idea. But his lips felt wonderful against hers. She leaned in a little and stopped thinking. He tightened his arms around her and after a long, sweet kiss, he pulled back and brushed the hair off her face. "Well, that was certainly worth the wait."

Paula just nodded.

"Sleep tight. I'll hopefully see you tomorrow?"

"I have Sunday dinner with the family tomorrow. But I'll be around during the day. If it's nice, I'd like to go to the beach for a while."

"Have you ever surfed?" he asked.

"No. It looks like fun, though."

"If I get some boards, will you give it a try with me?"

"Maybe. Probably."

"Okay. Good night, then. Oh, wait a minute." He pulled her back in for another kiss, a short and sweet one this time. "Okay, now we can go to sleep."

"Bye, Quinn."

CHAPTER 7

Paula drifted off to sleep dreaming about kissing Quinn. When she woke Sunday morning, her happy glow had faded, and she wondered if the kiss had been a mistake. It didn't feel like it at the time, but she'd been down this road before, and she didn't want to make the same mistake again.

She stayed in bed later than usual then slowly eased herself up, padded down to the kitchen and made a big pot of coffee. After pouring a cup, she took it out to her porch and curled up with the Sunday paper, which was already by the door. She didn't get the daily paper, but liked to browse through it on the weekend. She'd just topped off her coffee when she saw Hope step out onto her porch and wave her over.

"I have plenty of coffee made if you feel like visiting for a bit."

"I'll be right over." Hope went back inside for a minute, then returned wearing a comfy old sweatshirt and shorts. She helped herself to a cup of coffee and then joined Paula on the porch.

"Did you do anything fun last night?" Paula asked her.

"I went to dinner in Charleston with an old friend that was in town. It was nice to catch up. What about you?"

"Quinn stopped by the store yesterday, apologized and wanted to take me out to dinner."

"You went out to dinner with him? On an actual date?" Hope seemed surprised.

"No. I said no to that. But I did go over to his cottage to share leftover pizza and watch a movie. And we talked."

"About him not telling you about Bakey's?"

"Yes. He did redeem himself though."

"Oh? How?"

Paula told her about his plans to alter Bakey's menu.

"Wow. That's a big deal. I'm impressed."

"Yeah, I was very pleasantly surprised."

"So, you had a nice night then. What did you watch?"

Paula smiled. "My favorite movie."

"When Harry Met Sally? You got him to watch that? Impressive."

"He liked it. Or at least he seemed to."

"That's nice. So, the two of you are friends again."

"I'm not sure what we are." She was quiet for a moment, and then added, "He kissed me, when he walked me home."

Hope raised her eyebrows. "Well, that's interesting. How do you feel about it?"

Paula twirled a chunk of hair as she thought about the question. How did she feel about it?

"Conflicted, confused, swinging back and forth from wanting to do it again as soon as possible to wanting to run far away." She grinned. "How's that for all over the place?"

"Well, knowing you, and your history, that sounds about right. Sometimes long distance relationships can work, though. It depends on the people. Quinn's not Dan," she reminded her.

"I know. And it was just a kiss. I don't want to read too much into it, either. I'm guessing that Quinn's not looking for anything serious. And it does complicate things, given who he is." She took a sip of coffee and held on to the mug, savoring its warmth. "What if Bakey's still puts us out of business? I'll do everything I can to make sure that doesn't happen, but I have to at least consider the possibility. He's probably the last person I should consider dating."

Hope laughed. "On paper, it would certainly seem that way. But, you never know. His decision on the menu seems a good step in the right direction. Keep spending time with him, see what develops. Take it one day at a time."

"Is that what you would do?"

"Absolutely. It's not often that you find that spark with someone. I'd want to see what would happen."

"You're right. So, enough about me, what about you? Any new prospects?"

Hope laughed at the question. "What do you think? If there were, you'd be the first to know."

"Well, I think it's true what they say. You never know when you'll meet someone. It often happens when you least expect it."

"So, maybe I'll be pleasantly surprised one of these days." She stood up. "For now, I think I'll have a little more coffee."

Quinn called his grandmother first thing the next morning. He knew she wasn't going to be pleased with his decision on the menu. But that was an understatement.

"Have you lost your mind?" He had to hold the phone away from his ear because her voice was so loud.

"I think it's actually a good business decision, Gram."

"How on earth do you figure that? Please explain your logic."

"Well, you were willing to buy her shop right?

Well she and her aunt both made it clear they don't want to sell. This is giving them something that will likely cost you less than it would to buy them out. Cannoli are not a huge seller for us and she's known for them. And we have to employ an extra person just to handle wedding cakes, once that part of the business gets rolling. It's not our core focus. And it's what she enjoys the most."

"Ah, I see what's going on here. You have a soft spot for the niece?"

"Paula. Yes, I've been spending some time with her. I think you'd like her."

His grandmother sighed. "All right. I support your decision then. We'll see how it goes. And I hope to meet this girl sometime. Tell her my offer stands. I still think selling would be her best option."

"Maybe it would be," he agreed. "Why don't you come to Indigo Bay and check out the store when we open. You can meet her then."

"I might do that."

AROUND ONE O'CLOCK, Quinn knocked on Paula's door. He'd gone to the Surf shop up the beach first and rented two wide surfboards for the afternoon. The owner assured him they were the best ones for beginners. He hoped that Paula was still up for trying surfing. She opened the door and looked like she was ready for the beach. She had her hair in a ponytail and was wearing a tank top over a bright pink one-piece bathing suit and nylon shorts.

"Are you ready to go?" he asked her.

"As ready as I'll ever be. Have you surfed before?"

"Only since I've been here. I tried it out one afternoon and had a blast. It took me a while to get the hang of it, but it was still fun. Hopefully, I'll be able to help you so you won't have as long of a learning curve."

She smiled. "All right. Let's do this."

They strolled down to the beach, to where Quinn stacked the two surfboards by two beach chairs and towels. They each grabbed a surfboard and carried it to the water.

Okay, jump on and follow me. We'll paddle out a little ways and then try to catch a wave. You might want to to just body surf the first few times until you feel comfortable enough to try getting up. Quinn led the way and Paula followed close behind. The water was warm and not as rough as it sometimes was, good conditions for learning. They rode out, and then waited for the waves to come and carry them in. It was fun just body surfing in. When he glanced over, Paula was smiling as they caught a good wave. After three rides in, she wanted to try to get up. He showed her how he managed to get up and she tried a few times in the shallow water, to get the motions down.

"You ready to give it a go?" he asked, and she nodded. They paddled out and got into position on the boards. Paula got up fine, but as soon as the wave came, she fell right off. She surfaced, though, and rode the wave in the same way she'd done the first few times.

"It's harder than it looks!" she said when she reached him.

"It is tricky. It took me four tries to stay up," he admitted.

"Oh! Well, let's see if I can beat that." She grinned and jumped back on her board and they paddled out again. And she did beat his record, managing to get up on her third try. She was a little wobbly, but she stayed up the whole way and then she was addicted.

"That was great! Let's go again." They stayed in the water for about an hour before taking a break and relaxing in their beach chairs. Then they went back out for another hour before it was time to return the boards to the surf shop. Paula walked with him, dragging her board along in the sand. Once they dropped the boards off, they took their time walking back to get their beach chairs and towels. It had been a good afternoon.

Quinn was dying to kiss Paula again, but in the broad daylight, she seemed a little more reserved and it just didn't feel right. He didn't want to come on too strong and scare her off. He hoped that she didn't regret their kiss, but she was hard to read, so he wasn't sure. She was friendly enough, though, and seemed to have a great time surfing. He knew she probably wanted to be cautious and he couldn't blame her.

After all, he wasn't really a great candidate for a relationship, given all the traveling he did and when he wasn't traveling, he lived two hours away. Not all that far, but not convenient either. Not to mention that he worked for her biggest competitor.

She dropped one of the chairs and towels on his porch along with the one he was carrying.

"Thanks for the surfing lesson. That was fun!"

"Anytime. So, you're off to dinner with your family?"

"Yeah, we get together most Sundays. They look forward to it. I do, too. It's when we catch up."

A thought occurred to him. "Will your aunt be there?"

"Aunt Tessa? Yes, she always joins us. Why?"

"Well, I've been thinking, and I just wanted to throw this out there. I know your aunt said no to my grandmother's offer, but now that you're taking over—well, the offer still stands, if you decide you don't want to deal with trying to compete. It could be a win-win for all of us." He hoped that she'd decide to sell. He really did believe it would be for the best.

But as soon as the words were out of his mouth, he knew he'd made a mistake. A big one. Paula's eyes grew stormy, and she glared at him.

"Thank you for your kind offer and please thank your grandmother for me, too, but you can let her know that I'm even less likely to say yes, so you can stop asking." She walked off in a huff and then turned back with her hand on her hip and her face pale white. "Is that why you kissed me last night? To butter me up to say yes?"

His heart sank at the obvious hurt on her face. He'd bungled this, and badly.

"No, not at all. The exact opposite. I really was just trying to help. I'm sorry. Forget I said anything."

"I will, and I'll forget that kiss, too." She turned and walked back to her porch. He watched as she went inside and slammed the door behind her. He felt like an idiot. They'd had a wonderful afternoon, until he went and ruined everything.

PAULA WAS STILL STEAMING EVEN after she'd showered, changed and was driving to her parents' house. She should have realized Quinn had an ulterior motive. Getting her to sell The Sweet Shop was probably just another item on his to-do list. He'd seemed sincere when he swore that his kissing her had nothing to do with wanting her to sell. Maybe it didn't. But it still made her wary and determined to keep him at a distance. He was only going to be around for a few more weeks, after all.

She tried to put it out of her mind as she parked her car and joined her parents and aunt on their front porch. As usual, they were sipping their sweet tea. Her aunt must have just arrived as she was setting out a bowl of something and opening a box of crackers. She turned when she saw her.

"Oh, hi, honey. I made pimento cheese. You'll have to try it and let me know it's the best you've ever had, because it is."

"Mine is the best," Paula's mother corrected her as she slathered some cheese on cracker and popped it in her mouth. "This is pretty good, though," she allowed.

"All pimento cheese is good," Paula said with a smile. She poured herself a glass of tea and joined the others. They chatted for a while before going inside to eat, and Paula noticed that her father was quieter than usual.

"Dad, are you feeling okay?" she asked at one point.

"I'm fine, honey. Just a little tired," he said as he reached for a cracker.

"Your father had his annual visit with his cardiologist yesterday. They ran some tests. They have changed his meds and have him on a strict diet." She frowned as he reached for the pimento cheese.

"I'm fine. Really. I just need to behave more than I have been lately."

"I'm a little worried about leaving him alone while we're on the cruise. He doesn't always make the best choices. But he's promised to stay away from fried food, and fatty stuff."

Her father sighed. "All the good stuff is off limits for a while."

"Dad, I'll cook you some meals and leave them in the

fridge so all you have to do is heat them up. Healthy food that will still taste good. I promise!" Her father's eating habits were atrocious. He loved fried food smothered with gravy, creamy chowders and she-crab soup, all kinds of cheese. Her mother kept him in line for the most part, but Paula didn't blame her for worrying that he might make more bad choices while he was on his own.

"If you don't mind doing that, honey, I'd really appreciate it. Otherwise, I may be worried sick while we're away."

"Don't worry about me, Sarah. I'll be just fine. Paula will see to it."

"I will," Paula agreed.

"All right, then. Let's go in and eat. I made a nice roast chicken, broccoli and baked potatoes."

"Sour cream?" her father asked hopefully.

"No sour cream. You are terrible."

"Just checking." Her father winked at Paula as they walked inside and she laughed. She knew he was a handful for her mother.

After they ate, they sat around the table, chatting over coffee.

"Two weeks from now, you'll be on the cruise ship. You'll never have to get up to 'make the donuts' again. Unless you get bored and want to come help sometime. Barbara and I were just saying yesterday that we'd love that."

"I know, it doesn't seem real. I'm looking forward to relaxing on the cruise. When I get back, who knows. Maybe I will get bored and want to come bother you now and then."

Paula smiled. "Never a bother. I mean it. Anytime you feel like coming back."

"I'll keep that in mind. It's a big change for you. Are you looking forward to it? You could still change your mind. I could sell to those people if you want to stay in marketing," Aunt Tessa said.

"Funny you should mention that. As it turns out, Quinn, my new neighbor, the one renting, is the grandson of the owner and is here to open the store. He told me today that the offer is still on the table if I decide I want to throw in the towel. As if!"

Her mother and aunt exchanged a glance before her aunt spoke again. "It's not going to be easy. I was thinking it was time to retire soon anyway, so this was the nudge I needed. If it gets too hard for you, though, and if it stops being fun, it's always an option. I'm sure it wouldn't be hard for you to get a marketing job again."

Paula knew the market for people with her skills was strong and Maxine had also told her she was always welcome back if she decided that running the bakery shop wasn't her dream job, after all.

"No, it shouldn't be. And to be fair, he also said that Bakey's won't sell cannoli or wedding cakes. He seemed sincere that he doesn't want to hurt us. So, when he mentioned his grandmother's offer again, it made me think he just doesn't have faith that we can do it."

"Or maybe he was just passing on his grandmother's offer?" Aunt Tessa said thoughtfully. "If he's willing to take cannoli and wedding cakes off their menu, that's a generous step in the right direction."

"I suppose so," Paula agreed.

CHAPTER 8

Paula was crazy busy as usual all day at work on Monday and didn't come up for air until one thirty. She had a meeting set with Naomi at two to go over their clients lists, discuss the transition and make sure Naomi understood the different programs and ad campaigns that Paula had set up for each one.

Paula gathered up a stack of file folders and her laptop. She went into the conference room so they'd have room to spread stuff out and could be away from the phones which never seemed to stop ringing. Naomi was still out at lunch. She breezed into the conference room a few minutes past two.

"I'm so sorry to be running late. I just had the most amazing lunch with Quinn Jacobs. We went to Magnolia's because I just love it there. It's so elegant, you know?" Paula nodded in agreement. Magnolia's was a lovely and well-respected restaurant. A great spot for a business lunch. She didn't realize that Naomi was meeting Quinn for lunch, though.

"And he's such a gentleman! I tried to pay, using the company card, of course, but he wouldn't hear of it. He insisted on picking up the check. It made it almost feel like a date," she gushed. "I know it wasn't of course. But a girl can dream, right? He'd be such a catch. He's single and, well…loaded."

Paula smiled tightly. The last thing she wanted to hear about was Naomi's lunch with Quinn or her crush on him. But Naomi wasn't done talking about it.

"He loved all my ideas. And we're going to have such a great opening day bash. I've invited all the most important people in Charleston and Indigo Bay, of course." Paula had to admit that was a smart strategy. No doubt in their research they figured out that The Sweet Shop drew business from both areas. It would be a cocktail hour, after the bakery closes, with passed hors d'oeuvres, champagne and a jazz quartet.

"And Quinn agreed that it was a great idea to give every guest a to-go bag with a cupcake and a coupon to buy one loaf of bread and get one free. And of course one of the appetizers will be bruschetta, made on Bakey's toasted Italian bread."

"That sounds great." Paula's mind spun as she tried to think of ways she could use the party to her advantage. Maybe she'd run a sale of some sort that week, and have a big, bright sign made for the front window that would be visible to everyone who walked into Bakey's?

"So what do you think?" Naomi asked. She'd been chattering on while Paula thought about marketing ideas for The Sweet Shop.

"I'm sorry, I missed that. What do I think about what?"

"There's a big party later that week at the Charleston Society Hall. Their annual gathering. I don't know if you've ever been but it's really something, very exclusive. You have to know the right people to get an invitation." Paula had gone to that event once. It was when she was dating Dan and he went to network for his sales job. She hated it. It was such a snobby crowd, and Dan had abandoned her as soon as they walked in so he could go schmooze and Paula had been left on her own. She knew a few people there, but the conversations were painful as people name dropped and tried to one-up each other.

"I went once, a long time ago. It was interesting."

"Oh, I go every year. It's just marvelous. If I invited Quinn, I could make sure he meets all the right people and, of course, I'd get to spend time with him, too." An uncertain look crossed her face. "But, maybe that's inappropriate. I'll have to check with Maxine. I can say it was her idea!"

"Good luck with that." The conversation put Paula in a sour mood as she glanced at Naomi with her perfect hair and makeup, expensive clothes and elegant shoes. On her best day, Paula never managed to look so stylish. Maybe Quinn liked that? They'd certainly had a long enough lunch. Naomi was gone for two hours. Maybe he enjoyed her company.

She had no doubt that Naomi would quit her job in an instant and move to Savannah if Quinn wanted her to. He really was a good catch, if that's what you were after, someone rich from an important family. She wasn't into that at all. Clearly, she wasn't his type.

"So, I think that's everything, then? Is there anything we missed?" Naomi asked.

Paula looked at her stack of folders and her list of clients. They were all checked off. She pushed the folders toward Naomi. "No, I think we've covered everything. They're all yours now. Take good care of them."

"Oh, I will! I'm sorry to see you go, but I have to admit, I'm thrilled to get some of your clients. You have a great list."

"Thanks." Paula knew that she had a great client list. Part of her was going to miss working with them. The other part was eager to leave the agency world behind her and dive into this next chapter. The only thing she was truly nervous about was how the new Bakey's store was going to affect their business. She hoped that she could find a way to minimize the damage and maybe even find some new growth opportunities. She'd be lying though if she didn't admit it was a little scary.

"I think we're done then. I'm sure you'll do great!" Paula assured her.

"Thank you." Naomi's head swiveled like a squirrel when she saw Maxine walk by. "Okay, I'm off to talk to Maxine and see if she thinks it's a good idea to invite Quinn to the society gala.

When Paula got home, a little after five, the whole neighborhood was quiet. Neither Hope nor Quinn were home. She was feeling restless and decided to go for a run. It had been a long day, and she knew that being on the beach would lift her spirits. She changed into shorts, a tank top and her sneakers. She pulled her hair into a ponytail, connected headphones to her cellphone, turned on Pandora and set off jogging to the beach.

It was low tide, and the sand was packed down tightly the closer she got to the water which made it easier to run. She turned up the volume and ran for about twenty minutes along the waters edge before turning around and jogging back a little more slowly. She'd worked up a sweat and burned off her bad mood. Now she was feeling the runner's high, where all seemed to be right with the world. She was almost back to the path to their cottages when she spotted a familiar figure walking toward the water. It was Quinn with a fishing pole, a chair and a pail.

He looked up as she got closer and smiled when he saw that it was her.

"Hey, there. Want to join me? If I'm lucky, I'll catch dinner."

She laughed. "I don't think I'd be much help."

"You could talk to me and keep me company so I stay on the job. I might give up too soon otherwise."

"You don't seem like the type to give up."

"You're right, and I'm kind of hungry, and hopeful. Someone told me this morning at Sweet Caroline's that the fishing has been good the past few days."

"Well, good luck. I'm going to head home and hit the shower."

He flashed her his most charming smile. "If I catch something, will you cook it up for us? My fish cooking skills leave a lot to be desired."

She watched him fiddling with the bait and had a feeling he'd be ordering takeout. The thought amused her, and she smiled back.

"Sure, if you catch it. I'll cook it. But I'm not holding my breath on that," she teased him.

"What?! Sounds like you have no faith. I'm good at fishing, really," he insisted.

"I'm sure you are. If you're back in an hour with fish, I'll cook it. Otherwise, you're on your own and I'm heating up a can of soup."

He made a face. "That sounds awful. See you in an hour or less."

She laughed. "Good luck."

PAULA HAD JUST CHANGED into her oldest, most comfy pair of sweats and a long-sleeved tee shirt and was about to heat up some soup when she was surprised by an energetic knock at the door. She glanced at the clock. It had been forty-five minutes since she'd seen Quinn on the beach. She opened the door, and he stood there grinning and holding up a good-sized fish, cleaned and ready to cook. She laughed when she saw it.

"Congratulations! Come on in." He stepped inside and looked around the kitchen for somewhere to set the fish down. Paula reached into the cupboard, pulled out a platter and set it on the counter for Quinn to lay the fish down.

He set it down and then washed his hands in the sink.

"I was pretty sure that I was going to be ordering takeout. But just as I was about to give up, I felt the tug on the line. Can I help you do anything?" he asked.

"You could pour us a glass of wine. I have a bottle already open in the refrigerator. It's white wine, which should go well with the fish."

Quinn found the wine and got a couple of glasses down and poured for both of them. Meanwhile, Paula got busy with a large frying pan. She melted some butter in it and got out some flour to dust the fish. Once the pan was heated and the fish lightly floured, she put it in the pan to cook.

"You sure there's nothing else I can do?" Quinn sat at the kitchen table, watching Paula work.

She laughed. "No, this won't take long at all. I

have some broccoli I can heat up and some leftover cooked potatoes.” She took a sip of the wine and checked the bottom of the fish, which was already starting to brown. She flipped it over, added more butter to the pan and put the broccoli and potatoes in the microwave.

“This'll be ready in about five minutes.” She brought her glass of wine over to the table and joined Quinn.

"Are you sure you're hungry, though? I heard you had a big lunch,” she teased him.

Quinn laughed. "We did, actually. Naomi ordered a lot of food, appetizers and dessert. I guess she was hungry.” Paula guessed it was simply to make the meal and her time with Quinn last longer.

"Magnolia’s is one of my favorite restaurants." She smiled. “Naomi told me about the plans for your opening-day party. She has some really good ideas. It sounds like it will be a success."

"She's certainly enthusiastic. But it all sounds good. I hope you'll come to the opening night, too? My grandmother would love to meet you.” He looked a little uncertain. “Or would that be too weird?"

"It’s definitely a little weird,” she agreed. “But, it might be fun to check out the competition, and I would like to meet your grandmother too."

She got up to check on the fish. It looked perfect. She plated up some fish, broccoli and potatoes for both of them and brought the plates to the table. She grabbed forks and knives and some paper napkins and then sat back down again.

"Oh I forgot one thing." She jumped up and got a lemon out of the refrigerator. She sliced it into wedges and brought them to the table. She squeezed some lemon over fish and then took a bite. "Oh, this is wonderful. There's nothing like fresh fish."

Quinn nodded. "Thanks for cooking it. I could get used to this."

"Used to eating fish? Or to having someone cook for you?"

He laughed. "Both. But more than anything, I could get used to just being able to go fishing for dinner whenever I feel like it. I don't do this in Savannah."

"Savannah is on the coast too, though."

"It is. But I don't live on the ocean, not like this."

"I know. It's not the same. I lived in town for years before I bought this house. I love living right on the beach."

"I'm loving it, too. It's going to be hard to leave when my time here is up."

When they finished eating, Quinn helped her bring the dishes to the sink. She rinsed everything quickly and loaded it into the dishwasher. Once everything was cleaned up, she added a little more wine to both of their glasses and they went out to the porch to sit for a bit.

It was a gorgeous night. As they edged into the warmer months, the nights grew longer and the breeze softer. Out of the corner of her eye, Paula saw movement on Quinn's porch and a flash of orange fur. Mary was back. Quinn followed her gaze and smiled when he saw the little cat.

"I left some food outside for her, in case she came by and I wasn't there. She hasn't missed a day yet."

At the sound of their voices, Mary came scampering over and hopped into Quinn's lap. Paula could hear the cat purring from where she sat. She felt a pang of sadness as she thought of Teddie. She was starting to get the urge again to get another cat. Maybe, when Quinn left, if no one claimed her, she might take Mary in.

"Do you ever go to Savannah?" Quinn asked as Mary kneaded his leg, back and forth as if it was a mound of dough. Paula tried not to laugh at the sight of it, because Quinn was wearing shorts and Mary's claws must be digging into his leg, but he didn't seem to mind. He just kept petting her, scratching behind her ears occasionally. No wonder the cat loved him.

"It's been years since I've been to Savannah. It's funny because two hours really isn't that far."

"It's not. I'd love to show you around sometime, when I'm back there again. It's a beautiful city."

"I remember driving around with friends the last time I went there. We were curious to see that house from the movie Midnight in the Garden of Good and Evil. It was so pretty, right on one of the many squares. There's so much history there."

"There is. And lots of great restaurants, too."

"We went to a fancy place that was in a big pink house. I don't remember the name but it was really elegant."

Quinn nodded. "The Olde Pink House. It's great. But if you come, I'll take you to my favorite place. It's not as fancy, but the food is good Southern cooking. Paula Deen's Lady and Sons."

"I've heard that's really good."

Paula realized in less than two weeks, Bakey's would be open and she would be done with the agency and starting at The Sweet Shop. Big changes. She wondered if any of his other family members would be coming to the grand opening.

"Will the rest of your family be coming for the party?" she asked.

"My grandmother is the only definite. The others are doubtful. I'm really the only one that showed an interest in the company. Two of my brothers are attorneys, like my father."

"Oh, do they work with him?"

"No, my father specializes in real estate and trusts. Cody and Dylan thought that was boring. They work together doing a little of everything, whatever comes their way. Except real estate. They refer that to our father and he sends people their way, too. It works out."

"What does your other brother do?"

Quinn grinned. "Ever hear of the suspense author Travis Grundy?"

"Of course." He was one of the top selling

authors in the world. Right up there with John Grisham and Stephen King.

"That's my brother Travis. He likes to describe himself as a failed lawyer, because he went to law school, too, but after working at the DA's office for a year after graduating law school, he decided to write legal thrillers instead. It's worked out okay for him."

Paula laughed. "That's an understatement. I can't believe Travis Grundy is your brother. He's one of my favorite authors."

"He keeps a low profile. He tells everyone in Savannah that he works for Bakey's, too." Quinn sounded amused.

"He does? Why?"

"Travis has always hated being the center of attention. He doesn't do book tours or anything like that. He just stays inside and writes. We sometimes go weeks without seeing him if he's deep into a book. Confuses the heck out of my grandmother, as she's the complete opposite."

Paula laughed. "I'd love to meet your grandmother. I hope she decides to come."

"I think she might. I mentioned to her that I'd like to stay here a little longer and I think she's curious to find out why."

"If she comes to Indigo Bay, she'll understand why. Has she ever been here before?"

"Yes, but it was a long time ago."

Paula took her last sip of wine and yawned. The long day had caught up with her. She stretched and when she did, the movement woke Mary and she scurried off toward the beach.

Quinn laughed. "I wonder where she goes…"

"I don't know, but I think I'm about ready to head to bed soon myself."

Quinn stood. "I think that's my cue to leave." He handed Paula his empty glass of wine and took a step closer.

"This was really nice tonight, just relaxing and sharing a meal with you. Thank you."

Paula smiled. "Well, you caught the fish, so thank you."

"And you cooked it." He leaned in and whispered, "So thank you for that." He kissed her ever so lightly, as if he was waiting to see if she'd allow it. When she didn't pull back, he let the kiss deepen, and she found herself leaning into him. When he pulled back, he looked her in the eye and smiled again, the slow, charming smile that made her skip a breath.

"I just really wanted to do that. I hope you don't mind?"

Paula shook her head. "No, I didn't mind," she said softly.

"Good. Sleep well, Paula."

CHAPTER 9

Quinn had a feeling he might regret accepting Naomi Clark's invitation to the Charleston Society Gala. She'd mentioned it nonchalantly over the phone and stressed that the agency had an extra ticket they weren't using and if he was interested, Naomi would let them know and he could just give his name at the door. It was the kind of thing he knew his grandmother would want him to go to, so he said yes. He only wished there were two tickets so he could take Paula as his date.

Since the night he'd caught fish for their dinner, he and Paula had seen each other almost every day. They'd fallen into the habit of going to each other's house after work, sometimes sharing dinner, sometimes catching up a little later for a glass or wine or sweet tea, to just visit for a while and enjoy each other's company. On Thursday nights, they all went to trivia at the Surf Shack and on Sunday afternoons, they usually went to the beach.

He was aware, though, that the clock was ticking and his time in Indigo Bay was running out. He'd be staying for two weeks, maybe three, after the new store opened, and then he'd be back to Savannah and off to Kansas City. Normally, he'd be looking forward to the next project, but this time he wished the time would go a little slower. He was dreading leaving Indigo Bay and leaving Paula. He knew he was going to miss her. They hadn't talked much about what would happen then. He supposed that neither one of them really wanted to think about it just yet. It was easier to just take things day by day.

He heard a car pull into the driveway next door and knew that Paula was probably just getting home from her Saturday shift at the Sweet Shop. In two days, the shop would be hers, and the new Bakey's location would open. He had mixed feelings about it. He wanted the new store to do well, of course, but he was worried about Paula's smaller shop. He still hoped that maybe she'd change her mind about selling, though he knew that wasn't likely as she was excited to run the place on her own.

He checked his tie in the mirror. He'd managed to get it straight, which was a miracle. He was wearing his best suit and his favorite burgundy silk tie. His grandmother called it his power outfit. It fit well and he felt good in it. Ten minutes later, he walked outside and saw Paula sitting on her porch, sipping an iced tea while Mary was curled up at her feet. The sight made him wish that he could join them instead of going to what was sure to be a stuffy event. Paula waved when she saw him.

"You look sharp in your monkey suit! Have fun tonight."

"Thanks! I wish I was staying here with you and Mary."

She laughed. "You'll have fun. The food is always great at those things."

He smiled. "You up for surfing tomorrow afternoon?"

"Absolutely. See you then."

THIRTY MINUTES LATER, Quinn arrived at the address Naomi had given him. It looked like the right place. She'd described the building as a giant, pale pink mansion. The house was three stories, with soaring piazzas on each floor, columns out front and a circular driveway with several college kids out front parking cars. Quinn pulled his Jeep up, hopped out and handed the keys to one of the fresh-faced valets.

He made his way inside and gave his name to the two elderly women volunteers who were taking tickets. They checked him off the list, and he went inside and looked around. The event was a fancy cocktail party. There were tables along one side of the room piled high with different cheeses, crackers and fruit and waiters in black tuxedos circled the room holding silver platters with different appetizers on them. Quinn's eyes found the bar, and he went over and ordered a martini. He was amused when barely a minute after he got his drink, Naomi was by his side, all excited to see him.

"You're here! I'm so glad. I want to introduce you to everyone. Do you know anyone here?" The words came out in a rush. Naomi really looked like she was in her element. She was wearing a bright blue dress that hugged her curves and shimmered when the light hit it. Her heels were so high that Quinn wondered how she stayed upright. And the only word for her hair was big. Naomi had mentioned at their lunch that she was once Miss Charleston and he could see why. She had that look about her. Big hair, lots of makeup and teeth so white they were blinding. He thought of Paula snuggled up with Mary on her porch, her face free of makeup and her hair in a ponytail. He knew which look he preferred. But still, Naomi had been kind enough to invite him.

"You look gorgeous. Those heels are really something. Are they hard to walk in?"

Naomi laughed and lifted her leg to show off her five inch heels. He noticed that the bottoms of the shoes were red and knew from his sister and mother that it meant they were ridiculously expensive.

"I'm used to it. It's not easy, but they're worth it." She took his arm and slowly led him around the room, introducing him to everyone she deemed worth knowing. He recognized a few of the names and realized he'd met some of them at different events his grandmother had thrown over the years. As soon as Naomi said his name, they nodded and asked after his grandmother. And they all wished him well and promised to stop in the store soon if they weren't going to be there on opening day for the party Naomi was throwing.

One of the first people she introduced him to was Lucille Sanderson. She was an older woman, with a tiny dog named Princess that was peeking out of her tote bag.

"I know all about you." She peered at him over her glasses. "You opened right across the street from Tessa's Sweet Shop. I also heard she turned down an offer to sell and her niece is taking over the business." Her expression dared him to deny it. So, he said nothing and simply smiled as she continued talking. "But, I imagine that was your grandmother's doing." She looked him up and down. "What are you, about thirty-five or so?"

"Thirty-four."

Her eyes lit up. "I knew it! She fished in her giant tote bag of a purse and pulled something out and handed it to him. It was a business card for a woman named Maggie. "That's my great-niece. She's about your age, a little younger. You should call her. She's single and gorgeous, of course."

"Of course." He tucked the card in a pocket and

smiled. Naomi had had quite enough of Lucille, however.

"Lucille, it's been fabulous talking to you. But there's someone we need to catch up with. Talk soon!"

She whirled him away and by the time they circled the room, he'd given up trying to remember the names of all the people he'd just met. Naomi laughed at the look on his face.

"It's a lot to take in at once, isn't it? Would it help if I shot you an email Monday morning with all the names of the people I remember introducing you to? It might help when you see some of them Monday night. Quite a few said they are hoping to stop by."

Quinn was impressed. "Thanks, I'd really appreciate it."

"Of course. I'm happy to help. Are you hungry? We should try some of these appetizers that are making the rounds. The steak on the stick looks good."

"Sure," he agreed.

"Hold on. I'm going to go grab us some." Naomi took off and Quinn watched in amusement as she stopped one of the servers and loaded a selection of appetizers onto a small plate and brought it over to him.

"I got us some of everything. Help yourself."

Quinn picked up a beef skewer and nibbled on it while Naomi chattered on about all the various people she knew at the event.

"So, if you want to see any more of the city while

you're here, just let me know. I'd be happy to show you around." Her eyes held his a second too long and Quinn realized she was flirting with him. If he hadn't met Paula, he might have gone out with her once or twice to pass the time, but he'd dated girls like Naomi before. They were more interested in who his family was and the size of his bank account than who he was as a person. Because of his family, he seemed to attract a lot of girls like Naomi. Pretty Southern girls who were eager to marry well and settle down. He'd never felt the urge to do that, though.

That's why his job had suited him for so long. As soon as he started to get bored, he was able to move on to the next new thing. He knew that eventually he'd get tired of all the travel, but he didn't think it would be any time soon. He liked his life just the way it was. Although Indigo Bay was the first time he'd wanted to extend a stay.

"So, anyway, there's a new restaurant opening next week. We should go if you feel like it." Naomi smiled and held his gaze as she popped a stuffed mushroom in her mouth. She washed it down with a big sip of wine. "What do you think?" He realized her eyes were a little too shiny and her wine glass was now empty. He wondered how many glasses of wine she'd had and hoped that she wasn't driving.

"Next week is crazy with the store opening."

"Oh, of course!"

"Who did you come here with?" he asked casually, hoping that she'd say it was with a friend that drove.

"My roommate, Elizabeth. She doesn't drink, so she always drives everywhere. How lucky is that?"

He chuckled. "That's great." He glanced at his watch and wondered how soon he could leave without seeming rude. A few minutes later, he noticed people starting to leave and turned to Naomi.

"Well, this has been really great. Thanks so much for inviting me. I should get going though."

She looked like she was about to cry. "You're leaving already? Why so soon?"

"I have to be up early tomorrow. I'm going surfing with a friend." Never mind that it wasn't until after noon.

"Oh, okay. Well, have fun then." Naomi threw her arms around him, gave him an enthusiastic hug and then waved at a friend across the room and hurried over to her. Quinn shook his head in amusement and headed out to the valet to get his car.

CHAPTER 10

After a fun afternoon surfing with Quinn, Paula showered and then set about in the kitchen, getting ready for Sunday dinner. Her father was coming at six and on the spur of the moment, she'd invited Quinn, too, as they walked off the beach. She'd told him to come around six thirty, so she could have some time alone with her father first.

He seemed to be doing well with her mother gone, but it had only been a day. Paula was glad that they were only going to be gone for a week. She knew her father would have a hard time controlling himself without her mother around to keep an eye on him. That's why Paula wanted to have him over right away. She was planning to stop in several times during the week to see him, too, and bring food he could heat up easily—healthy food.

She put a spoon roast in the oven when she got

out of the shower. Roast chicken was his favorite Sunday meal and Paula was making all the side dishes he loved too, creamy mashed potatoes, green beans and fluffy dinner rolls with her special honey butter.

She was excited to have her father meet Quinn and a little nervous to see what he thought of him. She hadn't introduced him to anyone she'd dated since Dan. But, she wasn't making a big deal of this. She was going to just casually introduce him as the neighbor she'd been spending time with. She really didn't know what to expect once Quinn left Indigo Bay. They hadn't really talked about it.

At the sound of footsteps on the porch, Paula turned to welcome her father. He gave her a hug and handed her a chilled bottle of wine.

"I think this is the one you and your mother like?" It was one of Paula's favorite chardonnays.

"Thank you. Would you like a glass? Or I have a fresh batch of sweet tea made?"

"I'll take the tea, thanks." Paula poured a tall glass of the tea for her father and a small glass of the chardonnay for herself. The stove timer dinged. She opened the oven and took out a pan of hot dinner rolls and set them on a rack to cool. She then turned off the oven and put the roast beef and mashed potatoes in to keep warm until they were ready to eat.

"Let's sit outside and relax for a bit. I have some fresh cut veggies and hummus if you want to snack."

Her father made a face. "How about some potato chips and that French onion dip instead?"

Paula laughed. "Mom would kill me if I served that to you." She brought the veggie tray out to the porch and her father followed. He reluctantly reached for a carrot and dunked it in the hummus. "I suppose it's not too awful."

"Do you think you'll be able to stick to the diet while she's gone? I'll be by with some cooked meals for you." She knew he still went to breakfast at Sweet Caroline's most mornings and out with friends often for lunch or dinner.

"I'll try my best. It's not easy to pass up she-crab soup or fried chicken, though."

Paula smiled. "I know. How are you feeling?"

Her father beamed. "I feel great! I think that doctor was wrong about me. I've never felt so good." He leaned forward and with a gleam in his eye said, "I haven't taken my medicine in a few days. I don't think I need it anymore!"

Paula was horrified. "Why did you stop? Does Mom know? You're on heart meds, Dad. You don't just stop taking them."

"I didn't tell her. My prescription ran out, and I forgot to call in a refill and realized I felt fine without the meds, so I must be all better, right?"

Paula fought back a panicky feeling. "Dad, you felt better because the meds were working. It's dangerous to stop taking them. Please promise me you'll get the prescription refilled tomorrow. How long has it been since your last dose?"

"I don't know. Four, maybe five days? I'm not

worried about it, honey. I'm telling you, I don't need those meds anymore. I'm eating better and it's working."

Paula's mother would kill her if anything happened to her father while she was gone. "Dad, I promised Mom I'd keep an eye on you. Get the meds filled tomorrow and then when she's home, talk to her about how you feel."

Her father sighed. "Fine. I'll go to the drugstore tomorrow. Enough about me. How are you doing? Are you ready for your big day tomorrow?"

She smiled. "As ready as I'll ever be, I guess. Bakey's opens tomorrow, too," she reminded him.

"You'll do fine. Don't worry about that place. They're a big company. They don't know all the locals the way you do. They'll be loyal to your aunt's shop, and to you." Paula hoped he was right, but she knew that customers were often fickle and could be swayed by lower prices.

"I hope you don't mind, but I invited my new neighbor, Quinn, to join us for dinner. I think you met him a few weeks ago when he came into the store at the marina."

"Quinn…oh, right! He introduced himself and said he was here for a few weeks." He frowned. "Isn't he the fellow that is involved with Bakey's? I think your mother mentioned this."

"Yes. That's why he's here, to help with getting the new store up and running."

"Hm. And you've been spending a lot of time with this young man?"

"He's become a good friend. I wasn't planning to invite him, but we were surfing earlier today and he didn't have any dinner plans."

Her father looked thoughtful for a moment, then smiled and said, "You were surfing? Is that something new?"

"Relatively new. I've gone a few times now. It's fun!"

"Here he comes now, and there's a cat following him. He brought a pet on vacation?"

Sure enough, Mary was right on Quinn's heels as he walked the short distance between their cottages. She made herself right at home as she hopped onto a chair and sprawled out, keeping an eye on everyone as they talked.

"That's Mary. She's a stray cat that has been coming around. You remember Quinn?"

"It's nice to see you again," Quinn said politely. He handed Paula a bouquet of wildflowers.

"Oh, these are beautiful. Did you pick them yourself?"

He grinned. "I gathered them up along the beach after we surfed."

"I used to pick wildflowers for your mother," her father said, and chuckled. "That was a very long time ago."

"I'll put these in a vase. Quinn, what can I get you to drink? There's chardonnay, sweet tea or beer?"

"Beer sounds good, thanks."

Paula found a tall glass vase for the flowers and set them in the middle of the kitchen table where they'd be eating. She opened a beer for Quinn and when she went back outside, he and her father were deep in conversation. They were talking about fishing while Mary sat there purring loudly trying to get their attention. Paula went over to her and petted her, and the little cat was thrilled.

They chatted a while longer and then went inside to eat. Her father raved about the roast chicken and Paula told him she was sending all the leftovers home with him. After they ate, when all the plates were cleared and in the dishwasher, they sat around the table drinking coffee and nibbling on the cookies Paula had brought home the day before from the bakery. They were simple sugar cookies, but she knew her father loved them. She raised her eyebrow though when he reached for a third cookie.

"I know, I know. This is my last one. I swear."

"Barbara made those. They are good." Paula reached for a third one, too.

"So, big day tomorrow," her father said, and then added, "for both of you."

"It is a big day. But I know Paula's going to do great. The locals love your aunt's shop."

"Thanks. I'm sure Bakey's will do well too. People know the name and will be curious to check it out."

Quinn grinned. "That's what we're hoping." He glanced at his phone and then said, "I should probably get going. I'll be at the store early tomorrow." As Quinn stood to leave, Paula noticed that her father had gone quiet and looked unusually pale. "Dad, are you okay?"

He looked nervous and slightly confused as he said, "I'm not feeling perfect." A moment later, he slumped in his chair and Paula rushed to catch him before he fell. Quinn helped her move him off the chair to the floor. He'd passed out cold and when they moved him, his long sleeve slid up and Paula gasped at the sight of his arm. It looked like one long black bruise.

"I'm calling 911." Quinn placed the call. "They said they'd be here in a few minutes."

Paula's voice was shaky as she fought back tears. "He seems like he's breathing okay." She checked his pulse, which was faint, but steady. "He told me earlier, though, that he stopped taking his meds. He was feeling so good that he didn't think he needed them any more."

A few minutes later, the ambulance arrived and Paula filled them in on what she knew and that her father was missing his medication.

"We actually see this fairly often. Hopefully, they'll get your father back on track quickly," one of the EMT's said as they loaded him into the ambulance.

"I'll meet you at the hospital if you want to ride in the ambulance with him," Quinn said.

"Thank you. I'd appreciate that."

Paula rode in the back with her father and Quinn was a few minutes behind them.

They took her father right in, stabilized him and ran blood work and an EKG. When the doctor, an older man with graying hair and a no-nonsense manner came in, her father admitted what he'd told Paula earlier. The doctor's eyes were kind as he explained how important the medicine was and the danger of skipping even a single dose.

"This should be a wake-up call for you. You were feeling good because the medicine was working. If you want to keep feeling good, you need to take your medicine. Got it?" His voice was stern but Paula saw the amusement in his eyes.

"Does this happen often?" she asked.

"Yes. Your father is not unique in that regard. I do hope though that this is the last time I see him in here."

"It will be!" her father promised. Paula relaxed now that she knew it was just the missing medicine that was the problem. The doctor explained that the bruising on his arm was because he'd stopped taking his blood thinner meds and had been eating too much spinach. They gave him all his meds and kept an eye on him for the rest of the evening to make sure he stabilized. Just after midnight, they got the thumbs up to go home. And the in-house pharmacy filled all his prescriptions, so he could get back on schedule with his meds.

Quinn stayed with her, keeping her company and

talking and laughing with her father in the emergency room until they went home. They dropped her father off and got him situated at home before driving back to the beach. It was well after twelve at this point and she couldn't stop yawning as he drove. When they got home, he walked her to her door and gave her a quick kiss goodnight.

"Good luck tomorrow," he whispered.

"Thank you, and thanks for driving us home tonight. You didn't have to stay, but I'm glad you did."

He smiled and gave her a quick kiss again. "Of course I stayed."

CHAPTER 11

Paula got into the shop early the next morning. She was tired from going to bed so late, but her adrenaline was high as she walked in and said hello to Barbara, who was pouring a cup of coffee.

"One for you, too?" Barbara asked.

"Yes. I had one at home, but I need a second today." She filled Barbara in on the night before.

"Your father is a brat. I'm glad he's okay, though. That must have been a scare for both of you."

"It was." When she'd seen her father slumped over, badly bruised and unconscious, Paula saw her father as fragile for the first time and it scared her. She was glad her mother would be home soon. Though she was pretty sure her father wouldn't be pulling a similar stunt again.

"So, are we making anything special today?" Barbara asked.

"Yes. I've been thinking about what to do this week to offset the opening of Bakey's. I had a new sign made. Tell me what you think?" She went and got the cardboard cylinder she'd brought with her and pulled out the big pink sign she planned to hang in the window.

"Customer Appreciation Week, Buy one, get one free on all coffee cakes and loaves of bread," Barbara read the sign out loud. "Coffee cakes?"

"It's a new recipe I've been tinkering with. It's really good, and I thought it could be a signature item maybe. It's cinnamon walnut with a swirl of salted caramel over the top."

"Salted caramel is big right now."

Paula smiled. "I know and I love it. So, I wanted to try to incorporate it into something fun, but a bigger item than just a muffin or cookie. These coffee cakes are big enough to bring to a gathering or just have in the office or at home. And we're a bakery. We really should be selling more bread."

Barbara laughed. "We'd better get busy then." She made the donuts, then started on the bread while Paula focused on coffee cakes and cookies. A few minutes before they opened the doors, Paula hung the sign in the front window. She went outside to check the placement and smiled. The pink made the sign stand out. Hopefully the bright color and limited time sale would drive some traffic into the store. Even if it was just people who were heading to Bakey's. She'd take all the traffic she could get.

As she stood there, she heard a sound behind her and turned. The paper was being ripped off the windows at Bakey's and she gasped when she saw what it revealed. The store was beautiful and brightly lit, gleaming marble floors and shelves packed with every kind of baked good imaginable. There was already a line forming outside.

She went back inside and tried to squash the feelings of doubt and uncertainty that were rising. Could she really compete with that? Was she crazy to even try? When she went out back, Barbara took one look at her face, stopped what she was doing and came over to her.

"Why don't you take a break for a minute, before the first customers come in?

"If they come in..." Paula said.

"Stop that crazy talk. Of course they'll come in. I tasted that coffee cake—it's amazing. It's going to be a big hit. And I know my bread and donuts are the best in all of Indigo Bay and Charleston." That made Paula smile. She relaxed a little.

"You're right. I know you're right. It's just nerves. I got a look at their store and it's really nice."

"It's also shiny and new. People are drawn to that, but at the end of the day, they go back to what's familiar and comfortable—what they like. Don't worry so much."

"Okay. I'll try not to. Thanks for the pep talk."

"Anytime. That's what I'm here for. Now, let's unlock the doors and start selling."

THE REST of the day flew and Paula was surprised that they were busier than usual. A good number of customers came in after going to Bakey's first and then seeing the sale sign in the window. She saw a lot of shopping bags with the Bakey's logo on them. But she didn't mind as long as they were buying from her too, and they did. Quite a few took advantage of the buy-one-get-one offer and once she put out a tray with bite-sized samples of the coffee cake, they started selling like crazy.

What surprised her the most was that they sold out of cannoli earlier in the day than usual and several people mentioned that Bakey's had sent them over, saying that they didn't carry cannoli, but The Sweet Shop across the street did. And mid-afternoon, a young woman in her early twenties came in with her mother and said that Bakey's had referred them and they wanted to place an order for a wedding cake.

The overall money in for the day was only a little above usual, even though the units moved was more than double. Paula knew it was a bit of a gamble giving away so much, but she'd learned all about loss leaders in graduate school and sampling. Giving people something for free often paid off ten-fold when those people converted into regular customers. It also created good will and strong word-of-mouth buzz.

"Maybe we should come in earlier tomorrow?" Barbara said as they were closing up the shop.

Paula smiled. "I have more help coming in, so we should be okay. I hired someone with bakery experience to work part-time early mornings to help us get more stuff baked.

"Oh, that's wonderful, then. See you in the morning."

As Paula left, she couldn't help but notice that there was still a long line outside Bakey's. She'd noticed their hours on the door and they stayed open until six, which gave people time to stop in on their way home from work. Her aunt had always been adamant about closing the store early, long before the dinner rush, but Paula had been thinking about extending their hours. She almost didn't have a choice now. They stood to lose too much business by not staying open.

All in all, it had been a good day. She stopped at the bank on her way home and made a deposit then hit the shower as soon as she walked in. The Bakey's event didn't start until six, when the store closed to regular customers, so she had a few hours to relax and unwind before then. Quinn was just staying at the store, so she'd see him there.

After her shower, she was feeling so relaxed she decided to lie down, for just a minute. But just in case she fell asleep, she set her cell phone alarm to go off at five thirty to give her time to dress and finish getting ready. As soon as her head hit the pillow, she was out. She fell into a deep sleep and it felt like just a few minutes had passed when she woke to her phone beeping.

She was feeling groggy and slow as she eased out of bed and padded to her closet to figure out what to wear. She decided on a simple sundress. It was sleeveless with a white background and a swirl of colors all over it. It was bright and pretty and she felt good wearing it. Low heels and her favorite gold hoop earrings completed the look. She brushed her hair, added a touch of mascara and lipstick and then grabbed her purse.

She parked at the Sweet Shop and walked across the street to Bakey's. Naomi stood at the door, wearing an elegant black dress and checking off guest names on an iPad. She looked surprised and confused when she saw Paula.

"Oh, hello!" She glanced at her iPad, hit a few keys and then looked surprised again when she saw that Paula was on the guest list.

"You're all set. Go right in."

Paula stepped inside and looked around. The room was packed with people already and it was only a quarter past six. Employees walked around carrying trays of appetizers and various baked goods. There was a bar set up in the corner and Paula headed there.

"Could I have a chardonnay, please?"

"Why don't you try the sangria instead? I hear it's good." She turned at the sound of Quinn's voice.

"Okay, I'll try it."

The bartender handed her a glass of sangria and it tasted as good as it looked. White wine with muddled fruit and spices.

"So, how did your first day go?" Quinn asked.

"We were busy. I think we saw some traffic from people checking out Bakey's"

Quinn laughed. "Well, that's good for both of us, then." He took her arm. "There's someone I'd like you to meet." He led her to the opposite side of the room to where an elegant older woman stood sipping a glass of sangria and surveying the room.

"Gram, I'd like you to meet my next-door neighbor, Paula."

Paula held out her hand. "It's so nice to meet you. Quinn talks about you often."

His grandmother smiled and shook Paula's hand. "It's nice to meet you, dear. Quinn has mentioned you as well. I understand that you've recently taken over your aunt's shop as well?"

Paula smiled and stood tall. For an older woman, Quinn's grandmother was a bit intimidating. "That's right, as of today."

"Well, you've had an eventful first day, then. Thank you for coming by tonight."

"Thank you for the invitation."

"Now that the store is open, Quinn won't be around much longer. We have a new store opening soon in Kansas City." She looked thoughtful before saying, "He seems unusually fond of Indigo Bay. Usually he's chomping at the bit to get on to the next thing. He actually asked to extend his stay here. Did you know that?"

Paula nodded. "He mentioned that. He said he's surprised by how much he's enjoying living by the beach."

"The beach. Right." She smiled slightly as she lifted her glass of sangria.

Paula felt Quinn tense up beside her as Lucille Sanderson walked over. Lucille was dressed as she always was in a carefully coordinated outfit—her blue shoes were the exact same color as the collar on her small dog, Princess, who was sitting quietly in her pale pink leather tote bag. The dog was so little that only the top of her head was visible. Lucille was quite a character. The first thing she did was glare at Quinn.

"You haven't called Maggie yet!" Without waiting for him to explain she turned to his grandmother. "I told him a few weeks ago that he needed to call my great niece Maggie. She's perfect for him."

"Quinn never was one for setups. I've tried that before."

Quinn smiled. "Gram, we'll see you later," he said as they walked off.

"She's something, your grandmother. Very regal. Almost like a queen."

Quinn laughed. "She does know how to command attention." They both glanced over at her and she was surrounded by a small group who were hanging on her every word. Her face was animated as she looked to be telling them quite a story.

"I had a feeling she'd come. She said she was curious to see why I was so interested in staying longer here. I'm not sure she believed me when I said it was the beach."

"Well, what else could it be?" Paula teased.

"Oh, I don't know." He pulled her through a door and into the kitchen where they were away from the crowd and, for a moment, were alone. "Maybe it's this…" He wrapped his arms around her waist and brought his lips down to hers. She sighed as he deepened the kiss. She didn't want it to stop, but they both pulled apart at the sound of the door opening and one of the servers bringing an empty tray into the kitchen.

"We should probably get back out there," Paula said. She would much rather stay kissing Quinn, but knew he needed to mingle.

"I suppose so. Will you stay with me? This will be much more fun with you by my side. It's over in an hour or so."

"Sure. Is your grandmother staying with you tonight?"

Quinn laughed at the idea of it. "No. I offered, of course, but she said she wanted to get home to her own bed. She has a car service picking her up a little after seven."

"Oh, she's not staying until it ends at eight?" Paula was surprised.

"No, she said there was no need. She's right. Most people come early to these kinds of things."

His grandmother came over to say goodbye before she left. "It was lovely meeting you, dear." She looked at Quinn. "You should bring her to Savannah sometime." Quinn looked surprised at the remark but just nodded, and gave her a kiss and a hug goodbye.

Naomi came over and made a big fuss about saying goodbye to his grandmother, too, and Paula watched with amusement. The expression on his grandmother's face was priceless. It looked like she couldn't get away from Naomi fast enough. But Naomi missed it completely and came bouncing back to Quinn, gushing over how well the event was going. She looked surprised to see Paula by his side and even tried to take him away by putting her hand on his arm and saying, "Quinn, there's some people I'd love to introduce you to!"

But Quinn took a step closer to Paula instead. "Thanks, Naomi, but I'm done mingling. I think I've met just about everyone and if I missed them, I'm sure my grandmother talked to them."

"Oh, okay, then." She stood there for a moment looking back and forth at the two of them and then finally turned on her heel and ran off to chat with some friends. Quinn let out a sigh of relief when she was gone.

"She's…energetic," he said.

Quinn laughed. "You're being polite. She has a mad crush on you."

"Well, she should turn her attention elsewhere." He looked ready to kiss her in front of everyone and

Paula was smart enough to know that wasn't a good idea. "I should probably go. It's almost eight, and it's been a long day."

"Did you park across the street? I'll walk you to your car, then."

A few minutes later, they reached Paula's car.

"Now I can kiss you. I almost did it right in front of everyone. I wanted to."

"I wanted it, too, but one of us had to be smart."

He laughed. "That's no fun, though." He kissed her so long and slow that her head was spinning and her legs felt weak. When the kiss finally ended, she grabbed on to the door for support. His smile took her breath away.

"Good night, Paula."

CHAPTER 12

The next few weeks passed in a busy blur of activity. The new person Paula hired, Erin, was working out well. She helped Barbara with the bulk of the baking in the morning. Meanwhile, after a week, Paula hired two more front counter people and expanded their hours so that they closed at six, the same time as Bakey's.

She was surprised by how much business they did in that last hour between five and six. So many people stopped in on their way home from work. She'd started to experiment, too, with offering a few savory pies, like chicken pot pie and quiches, which flew off the shelves. They were a huge hit because at the end of a long day, many people just wanted to heat something up instead of cook a meal from scratch.

But still, their overall bakery business, the core items they sold the most of, donuts, cookies and cakes was down. She hoped it was a temporary thing and once people tried Bakey's, they'd stick with what they knew they liked. She was optimistic about the coffee cakes, though, as they were selling steadily. Bread sales were down, too, but she was less concerned about that. Bread was a strength of Bakey's and it had never been a big part of their business. Thanks to a steady stream of referrals from Bakey's their wedding cake business was up though.

When her aunt stopped in for a visit two weeks after Paula took over, she was encouraging.

"I think you're doing a fantastic job. You're not giving up and instead you're coming up with new ideas, like the coffee cakes and the pot pies and quiches. And staying open later. I've known for years that I should have done that, but I just didn't want to. I'm too old and tired to do any of it." She smiled and actually looked younger than ever. "Retirement agrees with me."

"I can see that." It was early in the morning, a little before eight and her aunt was on her way to a seniors yoga class.

"Well, I should probably go. It looks like you don't need my guidance here. You have everything well under control." Her tone was cheerful, but Paula picked up on something that was off.

"I've been meaning to ask you this. I don't know if you'd be interested, but I'd love to have you work part-time here, maybe a few afternoons behind the counter, if you're interested?" Aunt Tessa's face lit up.

Paula guessed that she might be missing the social aspect of the store.

"You know what, I'd love that. I don't miss the mixing and baking, but I do miss the people. All my regulars."

"Well, just let me know what works with your schedule and we'll do it. Plus, I'd love to bounce different ideas off you."

"I'd love that, too. Okay, I need to run. I'll see you in a few days."

WHEN PAULA GOT home that night, she felt a mix of emotions. It was Quinn's last night. He would have stayed another week, but Dallas had the cottage rented already. And his grandmother was eager to get him back to Savannah for a week before he left for Kansas City. She was sad to see him go and nervous for what that meant for their relationship. They'd still kept things light but they saw each other nearly every day and she considered him one of her closest friends now, but friend wasn't really the right word.

She wanted more, much more, and she didn't know if it was possible with Quinn. They'd lived in a romantic bubble while he'd been in Indigo Bay, but now she was going to miss seeing him every day, and with him heading to Kansas City it felt very similar to the kind of travel Dan did on a regular basis. But they'd both agreed early on to just take things day by day. That was easy enough to do while he was living here, but now it seemed more complicated.

For their last night together, they'd decided to just stay in. Quinn was bringing Chinese takeout, and Paula had stopped at the store on the way home and picked up some beer and wine. It was a beautiful night. The air was warm and slightly humid like it often was in the warmer months.

Instead of her usual casual jeans, she decided to dress up a little and put on one of her favorite sundresses. It was long and flowing with a pretty pastel floral pattern. She dried her hair and left it long and loose. She put on a little lipstick and mascara and the tiniest hint of perfume.

She heard his car pull into the drive a little past six and then his footsteps on the porch. When she opened the door, he just stared at her for a moment.

"You look beautiful," he said softly. "You always do, but this, this is how I want to remember you when I'm not here. In that dress, with your hair shimmering in the sunlight."

He set the bag of food down on the kitchen table and took her hands. She looked into his eyes and what she saw there gave her hope and made her miss him already. When he kissed her, she clung to him, wishing he was staying.

"We should probably eat before the food gets cold," she finally said.

He laughed. "I'll get the plates."

Paula poured herself a glass of wine. She opened

a beer for him and they ate on the porch. Within minutes of them settling on the rocker sofa, Mary appeared and after hopping up between them, instead of splaying out in the middle like she usually did, she pressed herself against Quinn's leg and looked up with a sad expression. He reached over to pet her immediately and the purring began.

"It's almost like she knows that you're leaving."

"I know. Makes you wonder sometimes how much they understand."

They stayed on the porch, long after they finished eating and their drinks were empty. Mary wandered off, and they moved closer together. Quinn put his arm around her and she leaned her head on his shoulder. They sat like that for a long time, chatting quietly and just being together and enjoying a gorgeous night.

"I'm going to miss you," she finally said.

He kissed her forehead gently. "I don't want to leave, either. I'm so used to seeing you every day. I look forward to it. It's going to seem strange."

"You'll be busy with work, though, and off in Kansas City soon."

"I hope I'll be crazy busy there, otherwise all I'll do is wish I was here. I probably will anyway. But, as wonderful as these past weeks have been. I have to remember, it's not how I live my life. I've never stayed in one place for long."

"Do you think that will ever change?" she wondered.

"I don't know. I've never thought much about it before. I like the travel."

Paula felt sad hearing what she already knew was true. His way of life was completely different from hers. What they had for the past few weeks was temporary, not real. It was just a vacation, for him. Now it was time to face the reality that what they had, as wonderful as it was, wasn't likely to continue. She didn't really see how it could. She sighed as she felt her heart threaten to break. She'd tried to protect herself and keep her distance but she'd still fallen hard, anyway.

"Will you come to Savannah?" The question surprised her. "I want to show you where I live and why I love it there."

"It's been so long since I've been to Savannah." She wasn't sure if this was a good idea if he wasn't planning on their relationship going any further.

He smiled. "So, you're overdue for a visit. I'd love for you to meet my family."

"Really?" A glimmer of hope began to emerge.

"Really. I'm just getting back into town tomorrow and need to give everyone a little time so how about a week from Sunday? I fly out to Kansas City that night and I'd love to see you before I go.

"I think I can make that work."

CHAPTER 13

The next week was long and empty. Paula was busy at the shop and glad to have Aunt Tessa back in the afternoons. Her cheerful chatter brightened the day. But when she got home in the evening and saw a different car and people in the cottage where Quinn had been staying, it was depressing.

It helped somewhat, though, that Mary seemed to have adopted her since Quinn left. The little cat was waiting on the porch every day when Paula arrived home. Mary was usually curled up in the center of the rocker. She would stretch lazily and meow and hop down when Paula stepped onto the porch. It only took a day or two before she won Paula over completely and had in-house privileges as well. She liked to run off for a bit after dinner, but she came home now at dark and happily slept at the foot of Paula's bed. Paula was glad for the company.

She spoke with Quinn briefly a few times during the week and while it was good to hear his voice, it seemed distant and far away. She was looking forward to Sunday, to see if they had the same magic outside of Indigo Bay as they'd had in it.

She set out Sunday morning around ten and arrived at Quinn's house a few minutes before noon. It was a gorgeous home right on Madison Square, one of the many squares in Savannah. Stately homes lined the grassy park area in the middle of the square. She double-checked his unit number, walked up the front steps and rang his bell. He came down right away, and his big smile and warm hug said he was glad to see her.

"Come on in. You'll laugh when you see my place. It's great, but it doesn't exactly have a lived-in feel."

She followed him up the stairs to the second floor and the door to his unit. Quinn had explained how he'd turned the old historic home into four modern condo units. When she stepped inside, she immediately saw what he was talking about. His unit was gorgeous, with floor-to-ceiling windows and a modern kitchen with stainless steel appliances and a sleek island topped with white granite that looked like marble.

The floors were gleaming hardwood and the furniture mostly black leather. It was beautiful, but the overall feeling was cold. There was no clutter, no anything, really. The condo almost looked staged as if it was really empty and the furniture just added so it would show well to a potential buyer.

"I've never liked clutter," he said as he watched her look around the room. "But, I'm also never here long enough to mess it up." He showed her around the rest of it, the master bedroom, small office and deck.

"A war was once fought there." He pointed to the square with it's beautiful Southern Live Oak trees draped in Spanish Moss. They were breathtaking, and gave a uniquely atmospheric look. "The history is what attracted me to this location. It's a convenient spot, too."

"It's lovely," she said.

He grinned. "You think it's sterile and cold. I can tell. It is, but it's home when I'm here."

She followed him back to the kitchen and he grabbed his car keys off the island. "Are you hungry? My grandmother is having a get together at her place. The whole family will be there, so you can meet everyone."

"I was hungry. But now I'm not sure. That sounds a little overwhelming," she admitted.

"Don't be intimidated. It was actually my grandmother's idea. She thought you should meet everyone and as she put it, 'see what you're getting yourself into.'"

Paula laughed. "If that was supposed to make me relax, it didn't work."

"Seriously, they're all eager to meet you. And the

food's going to be great. She had it catered from Paula Deen's restaurant."

"Okay, lead the way."

Ten minutes later, Quinn turned onto a private road that seemed to go on forever but was probably only about a mile or so. Hundreds of Southern Live Oaks grew over the top of the road in an arch pattern that took Paula's breath away.

"Pretty, isn't it? That's my grandmother's design. She's lived out here for as long as I can remember. We call her place the Plantation. It was one, many years ago. Now it's just a grand old house on many acres of land."

As they came around the corner, the house came into view and Paula's jaw dropped. It was a massive home, three stories high with wrap-around farmer's porches on all levels. There was a row of expensive cars out front—BMWs, Range Rovers, even a Maserati.

"That's Travis's car. He doesn't go far, but when he does he likes to go fast. And he has to spend his money on something."

Quinn pulled up next to the Maserati and parked. Paula got out and fought back the butterflies that were jumping around in her stomach. She was hungry and nervous to meet everyone.

They went inside and were greeted by Paul, the butler.

"Your grandmother has a butler?!" Paula whispered. She'd never known anyone who had actual servants.

Quinn nodded. "He's been with her for almost thirty years. He's like part of the family. And he makes a mean martini."

She followed him through the expansive main foyer, past the sweeping staircase to the upper floors, through the stunning chef's kitchen and onto a back deck, where it seemed the whole family was gathered. They were drinking iced tea and snacking on chips and dips while two caterers set up a side table and brought in the food.

Quinn's grandmother glided over to greet them. "I'm so glad you could come. Welcome to my home."

"Thanks so much for having me."

"Once Quinn introduces you to everyone and we've had a chance to eat, I'd love to show you around."

Quinn led Paula to meet his parents first. His father, Tom Jacobs, had gray hair and piercing blue eyes. He listened intently but was a man of few words, and just nodded and told Paula it was nice to meet her. His mother, Anne, was his opposite. She had short blonde hair, and a welcoming smile. She was warm and friendly and asked a lot of questions.

"How lovely that you live on the beach year round. Quinn has told us how much he loves it there. Did you grow up in Indigo Bay?"

"I did. My parents are both from the area."

"And you're an only child?"

"I am. I told Quinn he's lucky to have so many siblings. I always wished I had some," she admitted.

"Speaking of siblings, I should finish introducing Paula to everyone." Quinn pulled her away from his parents and over to a pretty younger girl with long blonde hair. She was texting someone on her phone and when she looked up, Paula saw she had the same blue eyes as her father and on her they were stunning. She was a very pretty girl with delicate ethereal features. She stood up and Paula was surprised to see that she was very tall and model thin. She definitely looked like an aspiring actress.

"Olivia, this is Paula."

Olive looked at her with interest.

"Is it true you went surfing with my brother?"

Paula laughed. "I tried to surf. He's much better at it than I am."

"Still, that's pretty cool. I'd like to try that some time." She smiled and looked at Quinn. "I don't remember the last time Quinn actually took a real vacation."

"Any luck with auditions lately?" Quinn asked her. Her eyes lit up at the question.

"Yes, actually. I'm going to Idaho next week for an audition."

Quinn laughed. "Idaho? Not LA or New York?"

"Adiel Bozeman is casting a new pilot that is filming on site in Riston, Idaho. At River's End Ranch. It's supposed to be gorgeous there and they are putting me up at the resort for two nights."

"That sounds so fun! I hope you get it," Paula said.

"Thank you."

"What's the part?" Quinn asked.

"It's a small role but it sounds fun. I play a guest that gets lost in the mountains and they have to send search and rescue to find me."

"Well, that shouldn't be too hard for you." Quinn grinned as Olivia smacked his arm.

Still laughing, he led Paula over to where his brothers were sitting around a big round table.

"Dylan and Cody are twins. They share a law office together downtown."

They both shook her hand and Paula thought it was interesting that they sounded so much alike yet looked very different. Dylan was shorter and dark-haired while Cody was tall, thinner and blond. They were both friendly and seemed curious to know more about her.

"And this is Travis." Paula shook the hand of his author brother. Travis also had dark hair and was taller and thinner than any of them. He had a wiry build and looked like he often forgot to eat. Paula could picture him hunched over his computer, banging out one of his best sellers.

"I've read all of your books," she said shyly. "I'm a huge fan."

"Wow. Thank you." He seemed surprised and pleased to hear it. For such a well-known author, he seemed surprisingly humble.

"Food's ready, everyone help themselves," his grandmother called out.

They sat informally around the large table on the deck. The food was very southern—fried chicken, black eyed peas, collard greens, mashed potatoes. It was all delicious and everyone went back for more. After they finished eating, Quinn's grandmother took Paula for a walk around the property, telling her about its history. She learned that the home had once belonged to one of the biggest rice producers in the area. When she finished her story, she was quiet for a moment before turning the conversation back to Paula.

"I hear that you're doing well with your aunt's store. We haven't gained as much market share as we anticipated."

"Our store has been open for many years. We have a lot of loyal customers," Paula said proudly.

"Yes, and that's wonderful. Now that you've taken over, though, are you sure you want to keep fighting? I made your aunt a generous offer and it's available to you as well, if you want to sell to us. You could do something else, with no competition." She smiled sweetly as they walked along.

Paula wasn't sure whether to be flattered or angry.

"That's very kind of you. I'm not ready to throw the towel in just yet, though. I'm enjoying the work."

"Very well. I just wanted to let you know my offer is still an option if you'd like to take it."

"Thank you." Paula wasn't sure what else to say.

"As you know, Quinn is heading off to Kansas City later today. He'll be there for three weeks and after that he'll be heading to Houston. I'm very fortunate that he's always loved the travel. You're very patient to put up with it." She looked at Paula closely.

"I didn't know he was going to Houston right after Kansas City."

"It's always somewhere. We are opening twenty new stores this year."

"He did say he travels a lot." Paula hadn't stopped to really think about what that meant. But twenty stores a year? That meant Quinn was going to be traveling non-stop. But it wasn't like he hadn't told her that from the beginning.

His grandmother stopped walking and looked Paula in the eye. "I like you. Quinn hasn't had a serious girlfriend in a long time. Not one we approved of, anyway." She started walking again and casually asked, "You've had long distance relationships before?"

Paula frowned. "Yes, once. I was engaged to someone who traveled a lot. It didn't work out."

"Hm. It's not easy. Well, shall we join the others?"

They walked back to the deck where Olivia was slicing a cheesecake with strawberries on it. Paula was too full to think about dessert. Everyone else had a slice, though. After a while, they said their goodbyes and drove back to Quinn's place.

Instead of going inside, they walked to the square and sat on a bench below one of the gorgeous Live

Oak trees. The sky was clear and sunny and the square was filled with people strolling by. Quinn put his arm around her and she leaned against him and sighed. In this moment, just being with him, she was happy. But she also worried about the coming weeks, wondering when she'd see him again.

"Your grandmother told me the company is opening twenty new stores this year. Sounds like you're going to be very busy."

He nodded. "That's true. It's always busy, though. We opened almost that many stores last year, too."

"And tonight you'll be in Kansas City." Paula couldn't imagine traveling the way that Quinn did. When she went on vacation, she was always eager to get home at the end of her time away. Doing it every month, while it might be fun at first, she knew she'd hate it. But, she also loved where she lived. She knew that made a difference.

"I'll call you once I'm settled in. And I'll see you when I'm back home in a few weeks."

"You won't be home on the weekends?" Paula knew that many people who were 'road warriors' traveled out on Sunday and back on Friday, spending the weekends at home.

"I do that sometimes, but not often. I'm usually only in an area for two or three weeks at a time, and it's just easier to stay there then fly home for a week or so in between openings."

"I see." But, she really didn't. It seemed like if it

was important enough, he could make it home on the weekends.

"What time is your flight out today?" she asked.

"It's at four." He glanced at his cell phone. "I should probably get going soon. Airport security is always unpredictable."

Paula stood up. Quinn walked her to her car and pulled her in for a goodbye hug and kiss.

"Thank you so much for coming here today. It has been a long time since I introduced anyone to the family, and I could tell they all liked you."

Paula smiled. "Your grandmother told me she liked me, but she also offered to buy The Sweet Shop again."

He laughed. "She means well, she really does."

"I know. I liked her, too. I enjoyed meeting all of your family."

"Drive safe. Text me when you get get home."

"I will. Safe travels, Quinn. I'll miss you."

There was something she couldn't quite read in his eyes as he leaned in for another quick kiss. "Not as much as I'll miss you," he whispered.

CHAPTER 14

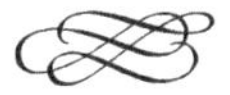

Except for a few text messages, Paula didn't hear from Quinn until Wednesday night. He called a little after nine and sounded exhausted.

"This week has been crazy so far. One fire after another to put out. Today it was an issue with the electricity."

They chatted for about a half hour, until Paula found herself yawning.

"It's great to hear from you, but I should go. I'm starting to fade and I'm going in even earlier than usual tomorrow." She and Barbara were still trying to fine tune how many of everything they needed to make each day. It was a fine line as they didn't want to be stuck with too many leftovers or be caught short.

"All right. I'll try to call again tomorrow. It's good to hear your voice."

"You too. Goodnight, Quinn."

Paula poured herself a glass of water, brought it into her bedroom and set it on the nightstand by her bed. Most times the glass was still full when she woke in the morning, but she liked knowing it was there in case she woke up thirsty. Mary followed her and hopped up on the bed. Paula set a small book over the top of the glass, so Mary wouldn't be tempted. For some reason, the water in that glass was especially alluring to her even though she had a full bowl of water available at all times.

She shut off the light and found that instead of drifting right off to sleep, her mind was spinning, thinking about Quinn and wondering what she was doing going into a relationship so similar to the one she left. She really liked Quinn, loved kissing him, and just being with him. But how was this going to be different from what she had with Dan? If she was only going to see Quinn on the occasional weekend, how was that a real relationship? She tossed and turned for a good hour before finally falling into a fitful sleep.

THE NEXT AFTERNOON, Paula was glad to have Aunt Tessa's help at the shop. Her aunt loved chatting with all the regulars that came in and seemed more relaxed and happier than she'd seen her in a long time.

"I don't have any stress now. It's just fun. You get to deal with all the not fun parts of running a business." Aunt Tessa laughed. "But, I know you have the energy and the smarts for it. I meant to tell you, I saw one of your ads for the shop on Facebook last night. That was fun to see. Do those ads do anything, though?"

"They actually do. Our coffee cake sales are up almost a hundred percent since I turned on that ad."

Aunt Tessa looked impressed. "And I thought people just went to Facebook to post pictures of trips and catch up with friends."

"They do. But while they're there, they see our ads."

"Isn't that something. How are sales overall since Bakey's opened?"

"They were down the first week, but I expected that. Bread sales are still down. Donuts are a little behind, but we've made up for the loss with the sales of the coffee cakes and the extra sales during the later afternoon hours. Cannoli and wedding cake orders are up. And the chicken pot pies are a big hit." She grinned. "I may take one home for dinner tonight, actually."

Aunt Tessa's eyes looked suspiciously damp as she got up and went to pour herself a coffee. "I'm really proud of you, honey," she said as she stirred in some sugar. "How is your former neighbor? I bet you miss having him there."

"I do. I talked to him last night. He's in Kansas City, keeping very busy with a new store opening."

"Will you see him anytime soon?"

"Not for a few weeks. I'm not sure exactly when. It depends how things go."

"I'm sure he'll be back before you know it," Aunt Tessa assured her with a warm smile as the front door opened and one of their regulars came in.

"Harriet! Did you bring pictures of that new grand baby of yours?"

THE NEXT TWO weeks went by quickly. Paula was disappointed that she didn't hear from Quinn as much as she'd hoped and each time she did, he was distracted and tired. He spent most of his time in Kansas City, running around solving problems, chasing paperwork and meet with the general contractor. But, finally the store opened and his work there was done.

"I'm looking forward to coming home on Friday," he admitted. "I'd love to take you to dinner Saturday night? I can come to Indigo Bay."

"How long will you be in town for?"

"Just a week. I'm off to Houston next."

"You're only home for a week?" A heavy weight of disappointment settled over her. Was this what dating Quinn was going to be like? Waiting for the one week a month that he was home?

"Quinn, I don't think I can do this," she said softly. It killed her to say it, but she'd been thinking long and hard since he'd been in Kansas City and she didn't see any other way.

"What do you mean?" His voice took on a higher pitch and she could sense his confusion and concern.

"I've loved getting to know you, but I can't commit to a relationship with someone that isn't here. It didn't work with Dan, and it's not what I'm looking for. I need more than that."

"What are you saying? Do you not want to go out on Saturday?"

"I do, more than anything. But, I can't. Every time I see you, I fall a little harder. It's better if we end this now, I think."

"Is it just the traveling? It's that big of a deal?"

"It's a huge deal, to me."

"Okay, let's think about this. I don't want to give up too soon. I'll call you when I get home, and we can talk more then? Okay?"

Paula sighed. "Okay, but I've made up my mind, Quinn. I don't know what you can do to change things, unless you stop traveling and I can't ask you to do that."

"We'll talk on Saturday. Sleep well, Paula." His voice was soft and sweet and it brought tears to her eyes. He was so perfect, in every way except the one that mattered most.

CHAPTER 15

"You've lost weight. Have you been dieting?" Hope looked at the jeans Paula was wearing, the ones that she hadn't worn in over a year because they were too snug. Now they were loose. She had dropped more than ten pounds since taking over The Sweet Shop.

Hope reached for the pimento cheese and spread a generous amount on a cracker. They were sitting outside, on Paula's porch. It was Friday night, about half past six, and they were relaxing after a long week.

"I forget to eat when I'm stressed, or busy." This past week, after telling Quinn that she didn't think they should keep seeing each other, she'd had no appetite at all.

"Did you eat today?"

Paula laughed. "I had some toast this morning and a cookie around three."

"That's not good. Is everything okay with Quinn?" She looked concerned.

"No, not really. I mean, he's fine, but it's just the travel. I don't think I can deal with it. He's gone even more than Dan was."

"He's not Dan, though," Hope reminded her.

"Oh, I know. But I know what I don't want, though, and I don't think I can be with someone who is gone that much. I want to build a relationship with someone who is going to be there."

"Does he know this?"

"He does. I told him it's just not working for me."

"I'm sorry to hear it. I understand, though. I wouldn't like it if someone I loved was gone that much, either."

Paula felt her heart twinge at the word love. Did she love Quinn? She'd tried so hard to keep her distance. But since he'd been gone, her feelings had only grown stronger as she missed him. And that scared her the most. That her feelings could be so strong, so fast. She knew if she saw him while he was home this week, she'd be lost, pulled in even deeper so that it would be even harder and more painful to end things.

"That's why I think it's best to end it now, before I fall even harder."

Hope smiled. "You're probably right about that." A minute later she asked, "Feel like taking a walk to the Surf Shack? We could get some fish tacos."

The Surf Shack had amazing fish tacos. Paula's stomach grumbled just thinking about them.

"That's a great idea. Let's go."

QUINN HADN'T SLEPT WELL since his call with Paula. He understood why she was hesitant to try to make a long-distance relationship work. She'd been honest about that from the start. Somehow, he'd thought that she'd make an exception for him. Which, he realized was arrogant and not at all fair.

He'd also found himself for the past week weeks feeling anxious to get home. That was something new for him. He'd never minded the travel before or been in any rush to leave. But, since he'd been in Kansas City, all he could think about was how happy he'd been in Indigo Bay. How much he'd loved being at the beach and with Paula. More than anything he missed being with her. He even missed Mary, the silly cat that had adopted them.

But, at the moment, he didn't really see an alternate solution. The traveling wasn't just a big part of his job. It *was* his job. He didn't see a way to do his job and keep Paula in his life. It was unfortunate and unfair to both of them. He sighed as his plane landed in Savannah. He was going to stop into the office to check in with his grandmother, work for a few hours and then meet up with his brothers at a pub near their office downtown. Travis was coming, too. He'd just finished a book and was ready celebrate with an after-work drink. Quinn was looking forward to seeing them.

CHAPTER 16

The shop was crazy busy all day Saturday. By the time a quarter to six rolled around, Paula was eager to lock the front door, head home, collapse on her front porch and relax with a glass of white wine and a romance novel.

The last customer left at a minute before six. She was on her way to lock up when the door opened and Quinn stepped inside, flashing his most charming smile.

"Hi, Paula."

"Quinn! What are you doing here?" She fought the urge to throw her arms around him. It was harder than she'd thought it would be to see him, knowing that they couldn't be together.

"I needed to see you. I missed you. Is there somewhere we can talk?"

"We talked the other night. Nothing has changed, Quinn. I don't know what there is to talk about?" She felt miserable saying the words and her eyes grew damp. She turned her face away so he wouldn't see as she fought back the tears.

"Maybe something has changed." She turned around and there was a twinkle in his eyes. He looked entirely too happy about something. "Were you going to head home? Can we have a quick drink on your porch?"

She'd couldn't refuse him. "I was heading home. Meet me there in ten minutes."

She finished closing the shop and drove home. Quinn was already there, sitting on the porch with Mary who was pressed against him, rubbing her head against his hand whenever he stopped petting her.

Paula unlocked her front door. "I think I have some of those IPAs left. Would you like one?"

"I'd love one. Need some help?"

She laughed. "No. I'll be right back."

A moment later, she returned with a beer for Quinn and a glass of ice cold chardonnay for herself. She settled onto the rocker and took a sip of her wine.

"So, what's new with you?" she asked, wondering what he was so excited about.

"I talked to my grandmother yesterday. And told her I need to cut back on travel. She thought it was a good idea. She never fails to surprise me."

Paula felt hope bubble up, but she was still wary. "How much are you cutting back?

"A lot. Eventually down to maybe ten percent. I'll work remotely and only fly out to sites if there's an absolute emergency. We're going to promote someone to take over the onsite work I've been doing and I'll supervise. I'll still have to do the Houston opening because it's already scheduled, but I'll only be there during the week and I'll be training my replacement. So, once Houston is up and running, I'll be back here for good."

"Really? You'll be back in Savannah?"

"Well, maybe not Savannah…"

Paula was confused. "Where then?"

Quinn grinned. "Here. With you and Mary, if you'll have me." He stood up, fished something out of his pocket and got down on one knee. "Paula, will you marry me? These past few weeks have been awful. I love you, and I've missed you more than I thought possible. I don't want us to be apart."

"You really want to get married? To me? Seriously?" Paula was babbling but she was completely shocked.

He laughed. "Yes, to you. As soon as possible. So, what do you say?"

"I say yes. I love you too, Quinn. So much." Her eyes filled but they were happy tears this time.

Quinn slid the very pretty diamond ring on her finger and then stood and wrapped his arms around her before lowering his lips gently to hers. They kissed for a long while and then Quinn smiled.

"I'm so happy to be home."

EPILOGUE

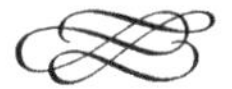

TWO WEEKS LATER, ON A WARM SUNDAY AFTERNOON...

"Would you like some more sweet tea?" Paula held the glass pitcher over her aunt's empty glass.

"Thanks, honey. I'd love some." After she topped off Aunt Tessa's glass, she did the same to Hope's and then her own before settling back on her comfy rocker. They were all sitting outside on her porch, enjoying the late afternoon sun. Paula was having her family over for Sunday dinner, and Aunt Tessa came by a little early. Paula hadn't seen Hope much since Quinn's proposal, so she invited her to join them as well.

"So, everything seems to be falling into place for you. You and Quinn and the store is doing well, too?" Hope asked.

"I almost feel like I should pinch myself. Quinn and I are doing great. He's off fishing, hoping to catch our dinner. I have some backup shrimp though if he doesn't."

"And she's doing a great job with the store," Aunt Tessa said proudly. "Business is up a little every day."

"That's wonderful!" Hope looked happy for her.

"You're next, Hope." Aunt Tessa smiled as she spoke and she looked so sure of it.

"What do you mean, I'm next?" Hope wasn't used to Aunt Tessa's grand announcements. She didn't make them often, but when she did, she was almost always right.

"Do you have a feeling about it?" Paula asked. She looked at Hope and tried to explain, "Sometimes she just knows things."

"Oh!" Hope still looked a bit confused.

"I just get these flashes sometimes," Aunt Tessa explained. "Don't know where they come from, but when they do it's a feeling of certainty that something will happen. That's what I'm getting for you. There are some things you've needed to work on?"

Hope nodded. "I suppose that's true."

"Well, your time is coming my dear. It will all be clear soon enough. Now, please pass the cheese and crackers."

Out of the corner of her eye, Paula saw Mary flash by, racing toward the beach. A few minutes later, she saw why. Quinn walked toward them, holding his fishing rod and pail, with Mary trailing along behind him. He smiled when he saw them on the porch and Paula caught her breath. His smile always did that to her and she imagined it always would.

"How'd you do?" she asked him.

"We're going to eat well tonight. I caught two big ones. I just cleaned them on the beach, so I'll put them in the refrigerator and jump in the shower."

"Oh, that's great! I can take them in if you want to use the outdoor shower." They usually liked to use that one when they came off the beach. Paula got up and walked over to him.

"Perfect, thanks." He handed her the pail of fish, then leaned over and surprised her with a quick kiss.

"What was that for?" she whispered.

He laughed. "Do I need a reason? Just because I love you."

She smiled, happier than she ever thought she'd be.

"I love you, too."

She took the fish inside as Quinn went off to shower. When she returned to the porch, Hope and Aunt Tessa were deep in conversation.

"What did I miss?" Paula asked as she sat back down.

"Nothing really," Aunt Tessa said. "I was just telling Hope to keep an open mind. Love often comes where and when you least expect it."

Paula thought of how she'd met Quinn, when he'd randomly rented the cottage next door. She'd never imagined how important he would turn out to be in her life.

"That's very true. I can't wait to see what comes your way, Hope. Let's toast to that." She lifted her glass of iced tea and held it toward theirs. They all tapped their glasses together as Paula said, "Wishing you all good things…"

I HOPE you enjoyed Paula and Quinn's story! Next up in this series is Hope's story, Sweet Beginnings, by Melissa McClone.

For an email whenever I have a new release or special sale, please join my reader's list.

Click here to see all the books in the Indigo Bay series.

ALSO BY PAMELA M. KELLEY

Nashville Dreams

Six Months in Montana

Mistletoe in Montana

Mischief in Montana

Match-Making in Montana

Winter in Ireland

The Wedding Photo (a friends to lovers romance)

River's End Ranch Series

Veterinarian's Vacation

Charming Chef

Cute Cowboy

Merry Manager

Bernie's Birthday

Missing Melissa

Billionaire's Baby

Teasing Tammy

Trust (Waverly Beach Mystery Series #1)

Motive (Waverly Beach Mystery Series #2)

ABOUT THE AUTHOR

Pamela M. Kelley lives in the historic seaside town of Plymouth, MA near Cape Cod and just south of Boston. She has always been a book worm and still reads often and widely, romance, mysteries, thrillers and cook books. She writes contemporary romance and suspense and you'll probably see food featured and possibly a recipe or two. She is owned by a cute little rescue kitty, Bella.

Keep in touch!
www.pamelakelley.com
pam@pamelakelley.com

CPSIA information can be obtained
at www.ICGtesting.com
Printed in the USA
LVHW041640160420
653698LV00019B/1980